D1279683

BETTER THAN GOLD

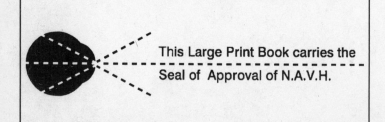

This Large Print Book carries the
Seal of Approval of N.A.V.H.

WILD PRAIRIE ROSES, BOOK 3

Better Than Gold

Laurie Alice Eakes

THORNDIKE PRESS

A part of Gale, Cengage Learning

GALE
CENGAGE Learning™

Detroit • New York • San Francisco • New Haven, Conn • Waterville, Maine • London

GALE
CENGAGE Learning™

LIBRARY OF CONGRESS CATALOGING-IN-PUBLICATION DATA

Eakes, Laurie Alice.
    Better than gold / by Laurie Alice Eakes.
        p. cm. — (Wild prairie rose ; bk. 3) (Thorndike Press large print Christian romance)
    ISBN-13: 978-1-4104-2442-6 (hardcover : alk. paper)
    ISBN-10: 1-4104-2442-1 (hardcover : alk. paper)
    1. City and town life—Iowa—Fiction. 2. Large type books. I. Title.
    PS3605.A377B47 2010
    813'.6—dc22   2010001870

Published in 2010 by arrangement with Barbour Publishing, Inc.

BETTER THAN GOLD

ONE

1876

SMALL-CAPS VALENTINE PARTY PERFECT STOP F PRO-
POSED STOP ACCEPTED STOP MARRYING
IN JUNE STOP

Lily Reese keyed in the telegram that had originated in Philadelphia and would speed along the wires from station to station until it reached its destination somewhere in Kansas. With each click of the code she knew well enough to produce in her sleep after three years as an operator, this kind of news never failed to thrill her.

Nor make her daydream.

Shivering in her tiny office to one side of the Browning City, Iowa, railway station, Lily imagined herself as the recipient of a proposal on Valentine's Day. She would wear a red silk dress, though it wasn't the best color for her blond hair, blue eyes, and fair complexion. Pink looked better. And

7

Matt Campbell would walk her home through a frosty night with stars blazing above like crystal beads. He would go down on one knee. . . .

All right, she didn't know him quite well enough to be in love with him or for him to be in love with her. Yet Valentine's Day had spoken of romance for so long, it might put the notion of working toward a proposal in his head.

The clacking of the machine yanked her back to the present. Since the last of her family had died three years earlier, leaving her completely alone and causing her to lose the farm, she had to earn her living, and that meant sending and receiving telegrams, not fussing over what had not happened on February 14.

This was February 15, and those crystal beads had not been stars. They proved to be frozen rain descending as ice so thick no one had attended the party Lily planned as an excuse to invite Matt to the house where she boarded. She wanted to impress him with her applesauce cake and excellent coffee. And her new dress. It was wool, not silk. It did, however, boast falls of fine, white lace she had crocheted herself. Yet one more Iowa storm prevented her entertainment and a chance to make progress with her romantic intentions. Now Matt had departed on the morning train and would not return for several days since he worked for the railroad and traveled a great deal.

"Lucky Matt." She sighed then concentrated on another message coming through.

ARRIVING AFTERNOON TRAIN STOP LOOK FORWARD TO MEETING YOU STOP YOUR LONG-LOST GREATNEPHEW BEN PURCELL STOP

Lily blinked. No, she was not mistaken. The message was indeed meant for Deborah Twining, the elderly lady with whom Lily lived. Mrs. Twining allowed Lily to stay in her small home's only spare bedroom free of charge in exchange for Lily performing most of the household tasks of cooking and cleaning. Lily owed Mrs. Twining so much, from providing her a place to live to the older woman using her influence in town to get Lily hired at Western Union — first as a messenger and then as a telegraph operator, despite her lack of experience. She wanted nothing to upset her landlady and friend. But this message could, coming so abruptly. The train to which the telegram referred was due to arrive within the next five minutes.

"Someone was asleep on the job." Lily frowned at the message. She could never get it delivered before the train pulled into the station. She should have received the message at her telegraph hours earlier.

"Why are you frowning, Miss Lily?" Theo Forsling, the ticket agent who also served as the porter, poked his grizzled head around the edge of the door. "Someone send you bad news?"

"No." At least she hoped it would not prove to be bad news. "Someone in Davenport must have been asleep at his station. This message was supposed to arrive this morning."

"Better late than never." The old man chuckled.

"I'm not sure that's true with this." Lily waved the flimsy piece of paper in the air. "It's about a passenger arriving —" The blast of a whistle interrupted her. "On this train."

"Good. Good. If someone is actu'ly arriving to stay a piece, they may need a porter." Grinning, he closed the door. Through the window, she saw him heading for the platform.

She also noticed Tom Bailyn, the owner of the new mercantile; Lars Gilchrist, owner of the other mercantile and the livery; and

Jake Doerfel, the newspaper owner and editor. The store owners were likely there to pick up supplies from the train. Jake met every train hoping for a story.

"And I have one for you." She jumped off her stool and dashed out the door. "Jake? Mr. Gilchrist?"

At her call, all four men on the platform turned around.

"I need someone to deliver this to Mrs. Twining immediately." She waved the slip of yellow paper in the icy wind pouring through the open-sided depot. "It's about her nephew arriving."

The train chugged around the corner at that moment, the squeal of brakes and hiss of steam drowning out her words. Apparently, however, she had said enough. All the men except for the porter jogged back to her.

"He's my new livery manager, you know." Mr. Gilchrist took the telegram into his sausage-sized fingers. "Didn't expect him until next week but makes sense he'd come before starting work. Things aren't quite ready for him, I'm afraid."

"But he's the new man in town?" Jake, not much taller than Lily, bobbed up and down on his toes, as though trying to make himself as tall as the two store owners. They

11

towered over him by at least a full head. "Single? Do you know if he's single? Is it true Mrs. Twining only learned of his whereabouts two weeks ago? Why didn't he ever contact her?"

"Please," Lily said between giggles. "They knew one another when Mr. Purcell was a child, but for the rest, you'll have to ask him or Mrs. Twining."

"You mean you live with her and don't know the answers?" Jake shook his head. "Don't believe that for a minute, Miss Lily."

"Maybe," Tom drawled in his rumbling baritone, "she doesn't think it's right to tell you private information about someone else."

"You're right, Tom." Lily gave him a smile. "I learned most of what I know from telegrams and from Mrs. Twining, so I can't breathe a word about it to anyone except her. And now that I mention telegrams, I must get back to my machine. Will one of you gentlemen be so kind?"

The station needed a regular messenger, as she had been when she first started working for the company, but no one had replaced the lad who had run off to hunt for gold in Colorado the year before.

"I'll be happy to deliver it, Miss Lily." Mr. Gilchrist patted her on the shoulder. "Don't

12

you worry about that. I walk right past her house on the way to the store."

"But if I take it, I can get some answers out of her." Jake reached for the telegram. "She's been a bit closemouthed about this nephew of hers."

"She told me enough to convince me to hire him." Mr. Gilchrist raised it out of the smaller man's reach.

Laughing, Lily retreated to her office. Through the window, she saw the three men still talking — or perhaps arguing — as they moved out of her line of sight.

She wished she could see the platform from where she sat. Although more freight unloaded from the trains than passengers, sometimes the travelers stepped from the cars and milled about to get some fresh air. On the occasions she was able to be outside and see them, Lily took in every detail of the ladies' fashions, from their hats to their gowns to their shoes. Occasionally she peeked at the gentlemen, too. If a handsome prince existed, he would have to step off that train to see her, sweep her off her feet, and carry her away to the bright lights and lively company of Chicago, Philadelphia, or even New York. Which city didn't matter so long as it had pavement, bright lights, and lots and lots of people.

She possessed high standards for the gentleman with whom she would someday share her life. He needed to be more than handsome; he needed to be entertaining, energetic, and a Christian.

Matt fit all those requirements except the entertaining part. He remained a bit too quiet around her. Maybe he was shy. No matter. She could fix that, and among others, one quiet person mattered less. He was fine to look at, and when he sang hymns in church, her heart just melted.

She glanced toward the window, again wishing she could see the platform. She wanted a glimpse of Mrs. Twining's nephew before he got into town and everyone else saw him first. If Toby, the young man who took the next shift, arrived a few minutes early instead of his usual few minutes late, she would be outside and on her way home in time to catch a glimpse of Ben Purcell, if not meet him outright. Meet the man whose existence could change her life and not for the better.

"Miss Lily?" someone spoke as he opened the door.

Lily glanced up at one of the railroad engineers. "Something wrong, sir?"

"Nothing serious. Just some bad track between here and Davenport. Probably ice damage. Will you send that back to Davenport?"

"Yes, sir, of course." Lily began to key in the message with the further specifics the engineer gave her.

"Thank you." He tipped his hat and headed back to the train.

Lily followed his progress. She saw no one in the depot.

She sighed. "Must have missed him. Now Becky and Eva will likely see him first." She frowned at her machine.

"Hey, and I'm even on time tonight." Toby shuffled in on feet that always appeared far too big for his spindly legs. "So what's the long face about?"

"I wanted to see someone is all." Lily hopped off her stool and snatched up her coat and hat.

"Mrs. Twining's nephew?" Toby took his place before the telegraph machine.

"How did you know?"

"Got hooked into delivering that telegram to her." He began to write his time of arrival in the log. "But you haven't missed him. He's still on the platform talking to Theo."

"Thank you." Lily settled her hat on her head with the aid of her reflection in the

15

window, bade Toby good night, then left the office.

Toby was right. The stranger still stood on the platform with Theo. She thought going up to him would be too forward, since he wasn't her relative. At the same time, she could hardly stay around the depot waiting for him to walk past.

She would simply head home at a leisurely pace and hope he caught up with her.

She must know how readily Mrs. Twining would accept him. Or prefer his company over Lily's.

Ben Purcell strode down the platform toward the baggage car. Stretching his legs after the daylong trip in the crowded railway coach felt wonderful. So did being in the fresh air. He inhaled. Despite the sting of coal smoke, the wind blowing off Iowa's rolling hills surrounded him with the crisp aromas of wet earth, animals, and open space. He smiled and stepped to the side of the baggage car, where a stocky older man prepared to heave Ben's heavy trunk onto the platform.

"Let me." Ben set down his valise and grabbed one end of the trunk to help the porter ease it onto the platform.

"What ya got in there? Gold?" The porter

cackled. "Not that anyone brings gold into Browning City. Some have come huntin' for gold over the years, though."

"No gold for me." Ben retrieved his valise from the platform, since it, not the trunk, held his worldly wealth in greenbacks, not gold. "I've come here to work."

"Yep. Thought so." The porter jumped from the railroad car and sauntered over to a handcart. "Need me to take that to the hotel for you? Your room at the livery isn't ready yet 'cause you're early. And Miz Twining ain't got room for you with Miss Lily living there."

Ben stared at him. "You know who I am?"

"Ben Purcell, right?" This time, the porter threw back his head and emitted a bellow of mirth.

Everyone on the platform turned to stare. Two big, blond men laughed, too, before turning away, carrying yard-high crates as though they were no larger than match-boxes.

Ben grinned. "You got me there, sir. How did you know who I am?"

"Everyone in town knows you're expected."

"I suppose they would."

If Great-Aunt Deborah told everyone about his imminent arrival, of course they would know. Ben hoped she had — and with as much excitement as he'd experienced every day since finding her address and then the advertisement for a manager needed at the livery. It was more than an answer to prayer.

It was a sign that the Lord said, "It's time for you to find your permanent place in the world."

"So is it the hotel?" The porter repeated his earlier question.

Ben still hesitated. He wished to meet his great-aunt as soon as possible — reacquaint himself, to be truthful. But twenty years' separation was a long time.

"You'll want to freshen up a mite before meeting Miz Twining." The porter gave Ben a sidelong glance.

"You're right." Ben headed down the platform. "The hotel, then."

"Mrs. Meddler will take good care of you." The handcart trundled in Ben's wake. "She'll —"

A hiss of steam and increased engine power drowned out the rest of the porter's words as the train accelerated. Railway cars slid past. People stared out the windows. A few people to whom Ben had spoken during the trip waved to him. He paused to wave back until the train picked up speed and the faces became blurs then disappeared altogether. Baggage and freight cars followed, speeding the passengers and goods farther west to more open and inexpensive land.

But Ben had family in Browning City. Family!

"How far is it to the hotel?" He turned to the porter. "Can you push that all the way?"

"I most certainly can." The man straightened his shoulders and jutted out his chin. "Been known to push two at once when necessary. You ask anyone about Theo Forsling. Strongest man in Iowa." He grinned. "Once upon a time. Won the plowing contest three years running before the rheumatism got into my knees. Mr. John Deere himself was here in seventy-one."

"John Deere himself, eh?" Ben held out his hand. "Then I'm honored to have you meet me at the train, Mr. Forsling."

"Ah, shucks, no mister to me." Forsling fairly glowed as he gripped Ben's hand in a powerful clasp. "I'm Theo to everybody in these parts. And speaking of these parts . . ." He released Ben's hand and shoved the cart to the end of the platform. "Better get a move on before we freeze where we stand."

"It is a powerful wind." Ben paced forward, his free hand shoved into his pocket.

With the train gone, fresh air swirled around him. He flared his nostrils to take in as much as he could. With every breath, he felt a little more of the city stink leaving his body. He had walked on Iowa soil for less than a quarter hour and already he could not understand why his father had traded the prairie for the road and city.

Actually for many cities, each dirtier and more crowded than the last.

"Like it?" Theo trotted beside Ben despite his claim to having bad knees.

"So far."

They left the depot. A skinny youth hunched over the telegraph machine waved to them. Ben waved back.

"Looks like Miss Lily has gone on home." Theo increased his pace on the road that headed into town. "But maybe we'll catch her up yet. Prettiest girl in Browning City."

"Lily." The name sounded familiar to Ben, but he couldn't place it at the moment. The one letter from his aunt had been full of names.

"Yep. Lily Reese, the daytime telegraph op — ah, there she is." Theo shot up his left arm to indicate a diminutive figure gliding along the road as though she stepped over a boardwalk rather than an icy street. Between a jaunty wool bonnet and heavy coat, blond hair gleamed in the twilight. Pale gold hair. Wheat gold hair.

"I see what you mean about hunting gold here," Ben murmured.

"Haw, haw, haw," Theo bellowed, slapping his leg.

The young woman stopped and turned. Her delicate features went well with her shining hair and fine form. She stood too far away for Ben to catch the color of her eyes in the fading light, but he guessed they would be blue. Sky blue.

"That yeller hair of hers ain't what I meant by folks hunting gold around here." Theo grinned. "But it'll do for a start. Step it up, boy; I'll introduce you."

"Yes, sir." Ben stepped it up.

Their footfalls crunched on the icy gravel. The cart trundled like distant thunder. A *crack* like a tree branch breaking under a load of ice echoed above the deeper tones of wheels and heels.

The last thing Ben remembered was feeling something slam into the side of his head.

TWO

With a shriek of horror, Lily raced back to the newcomer. She slipped in the frozen mud on the road. Her knee twisted, sending pain shooting up her leg. She ignored it and sprinted the last dozen feet to where the man lay.

"What happened?" She dropped to her knees beside him, wincing. "Did he miss his footing?"

"No, Miss Lily." Theo sank to the ground across from her with a creaking and popping of joints. "He was shot."

She gasped. "Shot? With what?"

"Rifle."

"Nonsense. We're too close to town." Her own heart racing, Lily touched the side of the stranger's neck, feeling for a pulse. "That was only a tree branch cracking under the weight of ice. Oh, praise God, his heartbeat is strong. He only stunned himself —" She broke off as warm stickiness soaked through her mittens. "Theo?" Her voice felt strangled in her throat. "He's bleeding."

"How badly?" Theo raised the man's head in one broad palm and probed with his fingers.

"Is he — did a bullet . . ." Lily couldn't form the right question in her mind, let alone speak it aloud. Despite her own misgivings regarding Ben Purcell threatening her role as the closest thing to family Mrs. Twining had, Lily didn't want him to suffer. Nor did she wish to be the one to tell the elderly lady that her sole blood kin was . . . dying. It would break Mrs. Twining's heart after so many weeks of hope and anticipation.

Tears began to course down Lily's face. The wind chilled them against her skin. "Theo —" She stopped again. She closed her eyes, deciding she was better off praying for the Lord to help.

"Cut a furrow right across his scalp." Theo gave his report in a soothing tone. "Stunned him, but he's not going to die on us."

Thank You, Lord.

Lily opened her eyes. "He'll die if we don't get him someplace warm and have the doctor see to him — sew him up or whatever is necessary."

She knew nothing of gunshot wounds.

Browning City was not the Wild West. Occasionally a farmhand drank too much and fired his gun, but that was more in high spirits than anything. Rifles were for hunting.

"We need to stop the bleeding." It was the only thing she could think to do. She yanked off her mittens and tossed them on the ground; then she opened her pocketbook and drew out her handkerchief — a scrap of linen and crocheted lace. It was an inadequate bandage at best, but it was all she had.

"I'll do it." Theo snatched the cloth from her and pressed it to the gash above the man's right ear.

So close. Another half an inch . . .

Lily swallowed a bitter taste in her throat. "I — I guess I can go run for help, but I hate leaving you here with some crazy man shooting off a gun."

"I'll be all right, and you can go faster than I can."

She could, and they needed help at once. Still she hesitated. She glanced from Theo's craggy face, a crease cutting between his bushy eyebrows like a river valley, to the stranger's smooth, strong features.

Her mouth went dry. She had seen some handsome men in her life, but even in repose, this man topped them all.

"Get going, child." Theo's voice held a chuckle as though he understood the reason for her hesitation did not stem entirely from her concern about leaving him alone with the unconscious man. "Mr. Purcell here will be catching an ague."

"So it is Ben Purcell." Lily sprang to her feet. Her knee threatened to buckle, and she grabbed the handle of the cart for support.

The cart.

"Theo, we can take him to town on this. I'm sure the two of us can lift him that high. Of course, we'll have to leave his trunk behind, but don't you think getting him to help is more important than possessions?"

Not that she would want her worldly goods left in the middle of the road.

"Good thinking." Theo rose. "Now you let me get that trunk down. It's mighty heavy."

Despite his protests, Lily assisted the older man in lowering the trunk to the road. Lifting Ben Purcell onto the handcart would be easy after the weight of his luggage.

She was wrong. He was a big man and a dead weight. No, not dead — limp. He would not be dead. Mrs. Twining had lost too many family members in her lifetime, including her children. Learning of Ben's whereabouts had brought her so much joy, it simply could not vanish before she had a chance to get to know him and appreciate him. *Not appreciate him to the exclusion of you, my girl.* Lily squashed the uncharitable thought, but it hung in her heart like a lead weight.

She must help him. Yet neither she nor Theo possessed the strength to get him off the ground high enough to set him on the cart bed even with a unified effort. On their second try, she thought she heard him moan. The third time, an outright groan emanated from his lips.

Perspiring inside her wool dress and coat, Lily set Mr. Purcell's feet back onto the road. If this were a big city, she could ask a dozen passersby for aid. Not here among the warehouses and silos between Browning City and the depot. At nightfall in the winter, with another train not due for hours, no one would pass by them soon enough to be of help.

"I'll have to run for help after all." She gritted her teeth in frustration. "We're hurting him. We can cover him with this." She unbuttoned her coat.

"No." The soft word from the wounded man cut through the air.

Lily jumped. "Mr. Purcell?"

"Not your coat." His speech sounded a little blurry. "Such a tiny thing. You'll freeze."

"Sir, I . . ." Lily felt her cheeks heat.

Theo guffawed. "Run along, girl. I think he'll do fine."

The buttons unfastened, Lily pulled off her coat and started to drape it over Mr. Purcell despite his protest.

He held up one hand and pushed it away. "I said no." His voice came out stronger, and he raised himself on one elbow. "Where's the mule?"

"Mule?" Theo and Lily asked together.

"The one that kicked me in the head."

"No mule, sir." Lily shook her head. "It was —"

Theo stooped again to slip his hands beneath Mr. Purcell's shoulders. "If I give you a hand, do you think you can get yourself into the cart?"

"If you can help me work out which way is up."

"That way." Lily pointed at the sky now growing darker by the minute.

"Funny." Mr. Purcell gave Lily a crooked, if somewhat thin-lipped, grin and pointed one finger at her. "Thought I saw an angel over thatta way."

27

Lily's cheeks heated. She didn't want this man to flirt with her. She wanted Matt to flirt with her, so she could care about him, not this stranger, this interloper.

Theo chuckled. "She is purty enough to be an angel."

"You're both full of nonsense." Lily pressed her cold hands against her hot cheeks. "I'm going to run ahead and warn the doctor to expect you."

"Why don't we take him straight to Mrs. Twining?" Theo eased Mr. Purcell to a sitting position. "She will be expecting him by now."

"Was going to the hotel." Mr. Purcell raised his hands to his head. When his fingers touched the gash, he grimaced. "Guess I do need a doc."

"He has an extra room if it's available." Lily feared it might not be with the cold weather bringing on the influenza. "Mrs. Twining doesn't have any space."

He could use your room, and you could stay with Rebecca.

Lily's conscience pricked her as she watched Mr. Purcell struggle to rise high enough for Theo to help him onto the cart bed.

"Of course he should stay with Mrs. Twining," Lily said. "She wouldn't want it any

28

other way."

Hoping neither man guessed her momentary selfishness, Lily turned and dashed down the road toward town.

Although no more than a quarter mile away, Browning City might go unnoticed to a nighttime traveler save for the scents of coal and wood smoke and cooking dinners in the air and the occasional flash of a lantern as someone performed outdoor chores. Businesses closed at supper time. In the winter, Lily arrived at work in the dark. If she had to stay late, she went home in the darkness, too. So she knew the road well. This evening, the wind drove the clouds from the sky, leaving it full of stars as she had longed for the previous night.

She welcomed them, too, though for a far different reason. She moved faster. In a few minutes, she reached the doctor's house on the edge of town. As she feared, someone with influenza and no family to take care of him slept in the physician's spare room.

"But if he's been shot, he needs more care than he'll get at the hotel, good as Mrs. Meddler can be." Doc Smythe shook his head. His glasses winked in the lamplight. "Shot indeed. Do they think we're in the territories or something?"

"I don't know. I guess I should tell the

sheriff, too." Lily shoved her icy fingers into the pockets of her coat. "But I'd better get to Mrs. Twining's first."

"You do that. I'll let the sheriff know when I'm done with the lad." Doc Smythe grabbed up his bag. "I'll just go out to meet Theo. Shot indeed."

Lily heard him muttering as he headed in the opposite direction from her. "Shot indeed," she said herself. "Nonsense."

Yet Ben Purcell bore a gash on the side of his head where something had furrowed across his scalp. Nothing but a bullet could do so much damage from far enough away that the perpetrator remained hidden from the road.

Lily suddenly grew aware of how the cottonwoods and warehouses made excellent cover along the road and increased her pace. Her knee throbbed. She bit down on the pain, lifted her skirts into her hands, and raced up the road until it turned into Main Street. Past Pine Street, then Oak; past the Gilchrist Mercantile, newspaper office, and the office side of the livery. When she reached Maple Street, she turned and fairly galloped the last block to Mrs. Twining's cottage. Breathless, she leaped up the two front steps, pounded across the porch, and yanked open the front door. "Mrs.

Twining?"

Her words emerged between gasps for breath. "Missus — oh, there you are." She stopped in the center of the parlor, her hand to her heaving chest. "There's . . . been . . . an accident."

At least she hoped it had been an accident and not some lunatic taking target practice on newcomers.

"Then catch your breath and tell me." Mrs. Twining's quavery voice and faded blue eyes conveyed calm and peace.

Lily wanted to sink down at the older woman's feet and let her talk of God's mercy and love until the panic departed.

"But there isn't time." She spoke her protest and regret aloud. "They'll be here any minute now."

"If you're referring to Ben's early arrival, that nice young man from the telegraph dropped off the telegram." Mrs. Twining smiled. "How glad I will be to see him."

"I'm not so certain of that." Lily bit her lip, reorganized her thoughts. "The accident — the incident involves Mr. Purcell."

"It does?" Mrs. Twining leaned forward in her straight-backed chair. Her lined face paled. "Is he — what happened?"

"We think someone was out shooting and hit him." Afraid the elderly lady would have an apoplexy, Lily grasped her shoulders. "But it's only a flesh wound. Theo Forsling is bringing him with the handcart. And the doctor has gone out to meet them."

"Shooting, you say?" Mrs. Twining stared at the window with its covering of white lace curtains. "Shot?"

"Yes. He should be all right, but he couldn't go to the hotel. . . . Mrs. Twining, should I get you a glass of water? Some tea?"

"No, no, thank you." Mrs. Twining shifted her shoulders, allowing them to settle in their normal, erect pose, and raised her chin. "Then we must see to things here. You won't mind giving up your room to him, will you?"

"They're already bringing him here." Lily headed down the short hallway from which one reached both bedrooms. "I'll clear out some of my things for him and pack some stuff to take to Rebecca's."

"It won't do. She lives all the way across town." Mrs. Twining followed Lily into the bedroom, leaning heavily on her cane. "You can stay next door with Mildred Willoughby."

"But . . ." Lily would not argue about how "all the way across town" was only six blocks and Mildred Willoughby next door would keep her up talking all night. Not to mention that Mrs. Willoughby would expect payment if Lily needed to stay more than a single night. Of course, she could not impose on Becky's family, either.

Oh, the depletion of her savings!

But it couldn't be helped. Mr. Purcell needed to stay with his aunt until the livery was ready for him. And Mrs. Twining would still need her around to help with the cooking and cleaning, which Lily already did to earn her room and board. The arrangement worked well for both ladies. Lily could save most of her earnings, and Mrs. Twining could remain in the house her husband had built for her more than thirty years earlier, before Iowa was even a state. Otherwise, she would have to go back east and live with her late husband's sister in Philadelphia.

Lily knew her choice in a similar situation would be Philadelphia. She knew no other land than Iowa, but how she wanted to.

Someday . . . if she didn't have to deplete her savings paying someone rent.

Her conscience pricked her again, and she returned her attention to Mrs. Twining.

"As soon as they get here," she said, "I'll go ask Mrs. Willoughby. Right now, I should get some hot water going."

She stepped back into the tiny entryway in time to hear the rumble of the cart's two

wheels on frozen mud and the murmur of
men's voices. She opened the door. Thin
streams of light from lamps in the parlor illuminated Theo, Doc, and Mr. Purcell. With
the aid of the two Browning City men, Ben
Purcell climbed off the cart and headed up
the front steps. Blood streaked the side of
his face and lay in a dark patch over his
shoulder.

Not a good way to meet a long-lost relative.

"Will you go heat the water?" Lily asked,
hoping Mrs. Twining would go straightaway
and not see her nephew in such a condi-
tion.

"You can do that, child. I haven't seen this
lad since he was knee-high to a grasshop-
per, and I'm not going to let a little blood
scare me off now."

It was a lot, not a little. Still, Lily would
not argue with her elder.

"Yes, ma'am." She backed toward the
kitchen, not wanting to miss the reunion.

Ben Purcell stepped across the threshold
to his great-aunt's house under his own
power. Though he appeared to waver a bit
and braced himself with one palm against
the door frame, he held open his arms. So
tiny she stood no higher than his chest, Mrs.
Twining rushed to him, cane thudding, and

threw her arms around his waist.

"My dear boy."

"Great-Aunt Deborah." He curved one arm around her shoulders and bowed his head.

Lily noticed his scalp now bore a white bandage. He still supported himself with his free hand against the door frame. She thought he needed to be lying down. Yet who would interrupt this moment? Certainly not she, despite the frigid air swirling through the house and chilling her face.

Her wet face.

She dashed the tears away with the back of her hand and spun toward the kitchen. She would not, not, not allow her own pain to cloud Mrs. Twining's happy meeting with her great-nephew. The death of Lily's remaining family three years earlier gave her no cause to feel hurt that the closest person to her had found a real relation.

Work. She must make herself busy. Occupation with her hands helped keep her mind away from thoughts she did not wish to entertain.

"I am not jealous." She set the pan atop the stove with more force than necessary. "Jealousy is a sin."

She dipped water from the bucket beside the back door and poured it into the pan.

She needed more wood for the stove and would now need to pump more water from the well in the yard.

"Miss Lily?" Theo banged open the kitchen door. "Doc needs some hot water."

"Soon." Lily emptied another dipperful into the pan. "Is he — will he be all right?"

"In a few days. Here, let me fetch you some more wood." He slipped out the back door and returned in a moment with an armful of short logs. "Doc wants him to rest here for a few days."

Only a few. Paying someone rent for a few days wouldn't set her back too far in her plans for escape from Iowa before the year was out.

But what would happen if Mrs. Twining liked having her nephew around instead of Lily? The older woman owed Lily nothing. She wasn't family.

Lily gnawed her lower lip as she poured hot water into a bowl for Theo to carry in to the doctor; then she set a pot on the stove for coffee. She disliked the idea of being stranded in Iowa any longer than necessary. Browning City was not home — was not where she belonged. It was merely a depot on her journey. . . . She hoped.

Her heart began to race as it had on the road earlier, and she opened the kitchen window for fresh air to breathe.

Room and board would take all of her wages if it came to that. She wouldn't be able to save any more, or so little she would be old before she got to the city. She would be too old to attract the kind of husband she truly wanted, a man who enjoyed social activity and bright lights. A man who enjoyed travel, like Matt . . . A man who could provide her with a fine house . . . A home to call her own.

But Ben Purcell didn't have a home of his own, either. He had intended to go to the hotel, since the room behind the livery wasn't yet fit for anyone's habitation.

"If it were ready . . ."

Able to breathe without effort, Lily closed the window and bustled around the kitchen, cutting slices of cake, setting out cups for coffee, checking the larder for something with which she could prepare soup for the invalid. Now her heart raced with excitement and purpose.

Tomorrow she would offer her services to Mr. Gilchrist to make the room behind the livery so inviting that Ben Purcell would want to live there instead of with his aunt.

THREE

The joy in Ben's heart proved powerful enough to counteract the pounding in his head. The latter, he knew, would go away in a day or two, though the scar would remain with him for all his mortal life. The former, however, felt as if it grew each time he saw his great-aunt.

"Family."

The six letters tasted sweet on his tongue —

Unlike the bitter medicine the doctor insisted he take for the pain.

One aunt wasn't much family to most folk, Ben supposed. It wasn't the wife and children for whom he daily prayed to come into his life. Yet one aunt in the form of Deborah Twining, whose faith in God seemed to be as powerful as she appeared to be frail, was enough for Ben's happiness to bubble up each time she thumped her cane into his room for an hour or two of talking about his mother and other relatives and discussing how he wished to settle in a small town like Browning City and get his own land.

Judging from the angle of pallid sunlight creeping through a gap in the curtains, Great-Aunt Deborah would arrive any minute with an afternoon cup of tea for each of them. Despite disliking the brew, he drank it to please her. Sometimes, Lily Reese arrived in time to prepare the tea. She never came into his room with his aunt, but he heard her voice through the door. The pleasure of remembering every word he heard her say occupied him during his waking hours of recovering from the gunshot.

Even as he thought about her, he heard her light, quick steps crunch up the front walk and click across the porch. He knew they belonged to her. None of his aunt's friends moved with so much speed and grace. Over the three days the doctor insisted he remain in bed, he learned each caller by her footfalls. He also knew Lily by her rhythmic rap upon the door. But he recalled little of her face, as he had not seen it clearly. He remembered golden hair.

"Golden hair and a silver laugh." Ben chuckled at his fanciful words, words much like those in the poetry books that had sometimes made their way into his father's peddler cart.

Listening to her speaking with Great-Aunt Deborah, however, he believed his thoughts weren't too far-fetched. Light and clear, her voice reminded him of sleigh bells. Perhaps she sang. . . .

"What does the doctor say?" Lily's voice came through with clarity as she stepped from entryway to kitchen.

"He'll be with us another forty years or so." Great-Aunt Deborah laughed. "But he can't go to work until the headache and double vision leave him. Which is more than all right by me. I do enjoy his company."

"That's unfortunate. I — I mean about him not being able to start work. Does Mr. Gilchrist . . ." Lily's voice grew muffled behind the kitchen door.

Ben closed his eyes. The mention of Mr. Gilchrist's name intensified the headache. He was supposed to start work in six days. Laid up as he was, he could not prepare his living quarters nor get to know the town. He had also missed church on Sunday. No matter what the doctor said, he would be in a pew on the upcoming Sunday and at the livery the following Monday.

He would be at the sheriff's office sooner.

The first day he got out of the house, he intended to pay the lawman a call and learn what he had discovered about the shooting.

"I won't let him in to see you," Great-Aunt Deborah had insisted in her cracked yet still firm voice. "He's come by twice, but Doc and I agree you need rest."

Ben wished he could disagree with her and get out of bed anyway. Weeks of working extra hard to pay for his move to Browning City and, before that, the grief over losing his father so suddenly seemed to be taking their toll on him. Not to mention the bullet across his skull and the rock on which he had hit his head when he fell. He had needed the rest.

With the rattle of the approaching tea service, he determined to remain out of bed all day tomorrow and be out of the house the day after that. If nothing else, he wanted to be well enough for his aunt to serve him the strong, dark coffee he smelled when Lily made it, instead of that bland brew from leaves.

He smelled coffee at that moment.

Do you prefer it, too, Miss Reese? He smiled at the notion and continued to smile as Great-Aunt Deborah entered the room with a teapot, cups, and slices of cake on a tray.

"It'll spoil your supper, but Lily insisted." She grinned at him. "Lily likes to feed people."

"A fine thing in a body." Ben rose and took the tray from his aunt. "Does she ever eat anything herself?"

"Yes, she does. She's been eating in the kitchen while I join you here." Great-Aunt Deborah lowered herself onto a straight-backed chair. "She'll join us when you're well enough to come to the table. But I think this respite from all she does for me is good. With her work at the telegraph office and caring for me, I think she doesn't have enough time to be as sociable as a girl her age should be."

Ben was still a bit bewildered about Lily's role in his aunt's household.

"What all does she do for you?"

"All those things these old joints of mine won't let me do anymore." Great-Aunt Deborah chuckled. "Which means just about everything but read. She cooks and cleans and does the shopping in exchange for her room and board."

Ben straightened, blinking against a bit of dizziness. "Then I should get out of here as soon as possible so she can have her room back. I have displaced your boarder, and it must be costing her something to stay —"

"Don't fret about that, lad." Great-Aunt Deborah shook her head. "She isn't suffering. And where would you go? The hotel?"

"The livery has a room, I believe."

"I understand it isn't yet fit for anybody to live there. Now eat some cake, or Lily will be disappointed."

"I wouldn't want to disappoint her." Ben took a slice of cake, though his conscience dampened his appetite.

He didn't like the idea of taking from Lily. Yet he enjoyed Great-Aunt Deborah so much, he didn't want to leave if she didn't insist. Despite her assurances, however, he decided that he had better get well immediately and set the quarters at the livery to rights so he could move in and give Lily back her room.

He could start this evening.

"I'm well enough to sit to dinner at the table now," he said, "if my staying in bed means she's been eating alone."

"Uh-uh." Great-Aunt Deborah leaned forward and poked him with the tip of her cane. "No getting up until Doc says it's all right."

Ben grimaced.

"None of that. You want to start work next week, don't you?"

"Yes, ma'am. But I'll be as weak as a baby

if I don't get moving around soon."

"Eat some more of this cake. Lily made it for a party we didn't have because of the weather." Great-Aunt Deborah slid another slice of cake onto his plate and set down her cane to pour tea.

He choked down the applesauce cake, which he knew should taste good, and the tea. All the while, he smelled coffee, and his mouth watered.

"Can I have coffee tomorrow, ma'am?" He felt like a child begging for a treat.

"May you." Her eyes twinkled.

He started to respond but stopped, his eyes widening. "You always did that to me, didn't you? Corrected me from saying *can* to *may.*"

"I did." Her face softened like crumpled tissue paper. "You were such a sweet but mischievous child that your mother never knew whether to hug you or punish you when you were naughty."

They sat in silence for a moment, Great-Aunt Deborah blinking away tears, Ben seeking memories.

"I was already six years old when she died, but I don't remember nearly enough of her." He shook his head, winced from a stab of pain, and sighed. "I never found so much as a picture."

"She was pretty. She looked like her grandmother — my sister — and you."

That made Ben laugh. "I hope I'm not pretty."

She laughed, too. "No, lad, you're handsome, and you probably know it. Why is it you aren't married yet?"

"No home for a wife yet."

"Mr. Twining and I didn't have one, either. We started our life together in a wagon."

"I can't wish that on a wife. Not after spending the past twenty years in one."

He wanted to ask her if she knew why his father had taken to the road for good after Momma died but kept it to himself. He wanted to talk of the happy times he couldn't remember of his childhood when he had family around him.

"You always were good with animals." Great-Aunt Deborah spoke as though she read his thoughts. "You spent a lot of time in the livery with your uncle."

"I seem to always remember horses around." He hesitated. "Why did he sell the livery?"

She smiled. "We were getting old, lad. Then some unsavory folk came through causing trouble around the end of the war, and Mr. Twining just didn't like the place anymore. He sold it to Charlie Jones, who turned around and sold it to Lars Gilchrist a few years after that."

"Why —"

"I'll go see how Lily is making out with dinner. She brought a nice piece of venison from Mr. Bailyn and is planning on a stew."

Ben's stomach rumbled despite the cake and tea.

"It won't be ready for another two hours." Chuckling, she headed toward the door, cane supporting her, she supporting the tray.

Ben sprang up faster than his head wanted him to and opened the door. He hoped for a glimpse of Lily, but the kitchen door stood closed.

"Maybe tomorrow," he murmured.

When Lily had to work late at the telegraph office the next day, Ben experienced a stab of disappointment. Great-Aunt Deborah and he ate leftover stew. Doc, however, gave him permission to begin going about his life: "If you take it easy."

The medical man sounded so stern that Ben said, "Yes, sir," and felt like saluting.

The doctor's instructions made little impact on Ben's actions. Immediately after Doc Smythe left, Ben donned his coat — washed and pressed, he noted — his hat, apparently retrieved from the road, and his boots. Protected against the cold, snowy weather, he departed for the sheriff's office. Despite the chilly air, several persons moved about their business. Some of them spoke to him. Many tipped hats in greeting. All of them gave him a second glance.

Ben smiled. He had spent too many days of his life as the stranger in a small town where everyone knew everyone else to mind about the looks of curiosity.

"Soon I won't be a stranger."

He expected they all knew who he was. The fact of someone shooting at him upon his arrival would make him even more of an oddity than the average stranger strolling through town.

His head clearing for the first time since he stepped into that flying lead, Ben paused in the middle of the Main Street boardwalk and frowned. He'd known the sheriff wanted to speak with him about the shooting but figured the lawman simply wanted to know if Ben had seen anything that could identify the gunman.

Ben didn't believe for a minute that he had been the intended target of the shooting. He hoped the sheriff and others didn't think that of him, either. The notion would make life uncomfortable for Great-Aunt

Deborah. People might even think he should leave town.

His quick prayer failed to lighten his heavy heart before he reached the sheriff's office. Taking a deep breath, Ben opened the thick wooden door and stepped inside.

Heat, the aroma of wood smoke and strong coffee, and a tuneless humming somewhere in another room met him inside. So did the surprisingly young man wearing the sheriff's badge and seated with his feet propped on the desk.

"How may I help you?" He had a deep, rich voice that seemed at odds with his cherubic countenance.

"I'm Ben Purcell." Ben held out his hand.

"About time." The sheriff swung his feet to the floor and rose. "You should have been in here four days ago."

Ben did not respond and withdrew his hand. The man knew why he hadn't been.

"Name's Dodd. Billy Dodd. Have a seat. Coffee?"

"Yes, thank you."

Deciding the man was friendlier than his words had first implied, Ben lowered himself onto the other chair. "I suppose you don't have much crime here, do you?"

It seemed a good topic for conversing with a lawman.

"No, sir." Dodd chuckled. "I work at a saddler half my time. That's why old Sheriff Morton moved on. Bored here." He poured coffee from a pot simmering on the stove into two thick mugs and carried them to the desk. "That's why I wanted to talk to you. People just don't get shot around here."

"I don't get shot around anywhere." Ben smiled.

"Humph." Dodd slid onto his chair and propped his elbows on the desk. "Funny thing that, you coming into town and getting hit straight off. Sure you didn't bring an enemy along?"

"Sheriff Dodd, sir . . ." Ben paused, choosing his words with care. "I don't have many friends. Never stayed in one place long enough to make and keep them. But the same goes for enemies. As far as I know, I don't have any of those."

"I can only take your word for that." Dodd blew across the top of his coffee. "But in these parts, we're inclined to take a man's word. And you are Miz Twining's nephew or something, aren't you?"

"Great-nephew, yes."

"Mm-hmm." Dodd nodded. "That counts for something. We all think the world of her. So if she vouches for you, you stay."

Ben raised his eyebrows. "And if she

didn't?"

"We don't want crime in this town. Hasn't been any since those train robbers rode in here and tried to settle right after the war."

Gold. Ben recalled Great-Aunt Deborah mentioning trouble coming to town and having something to do with the livery.

"I mean," Dodd added, "sometimes a youth gets ahold of some rotgut and kicks up a ruckus, and we have an occasional stealing of a horse or cow, but that's all it is. Boring, but we like it that way."

"I can understand why."

Ben had experienced too many weeks in cities where one never left so much as an apple unattended or it disappeared.

"So we want to catch the man who did this to Miz Twining's nephew." Dodd's forehead creased with his frown. "Any ideas?"

Ben shook his head. A few stars floated before his eyes. "No idea. I didn't see a thing. It was getting dark and . . ."

At the memory of seeing the small, female form ahead of him, he felt his neck grow warm under his collar.

"I wasn't looking for anyone. Just talking to Theo and — boom." He touched the side of his head.

"Hmm." Dodd's badge rose and fell with

his sigh. "Thought maybe you'd remember something. It's just such a strange thing."

"Yes, sir, it is." Ben reckoned his coffee was cool enough to drink and took a sip. It was as thick as mud and tasted as rich as molasses after all the tea he'd had lately. "Sorry I can't be of more help."

"Not your fault. But maybe you can tell me where you're from and why it took you so long to come to Miz Twining after she was widowed."

"I'm from here." Ben settled back in his chair, coffee cup in hand. "My parents had a farm a long time ago; then Momma died and Pa took to the roads and me along with him. I didn't remember much about my family until Pa died and I went through his papers. I found some old letters from Deborah Twining and thought she might be my mother's aunt, so I sent a telegram here to see if she was still around."

"Such a pity. My folks have been here for over thirty years, and my wife's folks have been here nearly as long. Iowa wasn't even a state yet, and they had it rough, but it's paid off. We're settled for good."

"I'd like that."

"If you're telling me the truth about not having enemies here, then you're welcome to stay. We still need folks to settle and help

51

this town prosper."

"I'm telling the truth." Ben took care not to let his annoyance show in his voice.

Although Dodd continued in a friendly manner, Ben finished his coffee and departed from the office as quickly as he could without being impolite, for he couldn't shake the notion that the sheriff didn't quite believe him.

Thoughtful about why the man would doubt him despite saying that the town would accept Deborah Twining's great-nephew, Ben stepped from the heat to the cold and came face-to-face with Lily Reese.

Seeing her by the light of day, even the gray light from the clouds, Ben knew he wouldn't forget any detail now. With eyes the color of an October sky and hair the color of wheat, smooth, creamy skin, and a straight, slim nose, she appeared as delicate as the flower for which she was named. His mouth went dry, and words clogged his throat.

"Good afternoon, Mr. Purcell." She gave him a smile that curled his toes up inside his boots. "I'm glad to see you about."

"I am, too. I mean, I'm glad to be about." Now his ears burned.

"May I walk you somewhere, Miss Reese?"

The offer was bold, since they hadn't been properly introduced, but he had listened to her voice for days and felt like he knew her.

"Thank you for asking, but I need to rush off." She began to move away from him as she spoke. "I begged Toby to come in and work at the telegraph office for an hour so I could reach the mercantile. It always closes before I finish work."

"I should be on my way to the mercantile myself." Ben fell into step beside her. "I need to tell Mr. Gilchrist that I can start work on Monday."

"I'm pleased to hear that." She glanced over her shoulder. "I see you finally met the sheriff."

"Yes, ma'am, I did."

Lily laughed. "You expected someone older and wiser?"

"I think I did."

Ben wanted to change the subject. He didn't want to speak of how the sheriff seemed not to believe him regarding his lack of enemies. He glanced about, seeking another topic of conversation, and caught sight of a patch of ice right in front of them from where a shop's eaves had dripped onto the walk.

"Have a care." He slipped one hand beneath her elbow to support her.

She pulled her arm away so fast she slid on the frozen patch.

He grasped her arm again, steadying her. "I warned you to have a care." He made his tone light and teasing and smiled down at her.

She stood motionless, looking up at him with alarm clouding her eyes and turning down the corners of her mouth.

He felt like she looked — dazed.

"I need to hurry." Her voice sounded hoarse, not at all her usual clear tones.

He nodded and released her. "I'd better let you. I'm not as quick as I'd like to be quite yet. We can talk some tonight at my aunt's house."

But Lily didn't arrive at Great-Aunt Deborah's house that night.

"She sent a note saying she was working late, that Theo would walk her home and she would eat with her friend Becky," Great-Aunt Deborah explained. "Will you get that chicken off the stove? I can put it into the pot, but I can't lift it once it's filled with meat and stock."

Ben moved the stewed chicken from the stove. "You sit down. I'll serve up."

Once they were seated with plates of fragrant chicken and biscuits and he had asked the blessing over the food, Ben brought up the subject of Miss Lily Reese again.

"I ran into her today when I came out of the sheriff's office."

"In the middle of the day?" Great-Aunt Deborah forked up some peas but didn't eat them. "That's odd."

Nothing was as odd or disturbing to his heart as the jolt he'd felt when he held her arm tightly enough to keep her from falling. Before, he had only experienced that sensation when he'd found himself too close to a lightning strike.

And Lily had felt it, too. At least Ben presumed she did from that expression of dismay on her face.

"I wonder why she wasn't working," Great-Aunt Deborah said.

"She was headed to the mercantile. Someone named Toby was working for her for an hour, she said."

"Ah." His aunt still looked thoughtful as she resumed eating. "Did you go see Mr. Gilchrist?"

"I'll go tomorrow. Miss Lily was headed there, so I thought I'd wait."

Great-Aunt Deborah's snowy eyebrows arched. "Didn't you want to walk with her?"

"More than anything. I mean" — he laughed — "yes, ma'am, I thought it would be a fine thing to do, especially since the walk was icy. But she seemed in a hurry."

"Lily is always in a hurry. You need to run to keep up with her. But . . ." She paused for several bites, so long that Ben could barely stop himself from demanding she continue. At last, she set down her fork and folded her hands on the edge of the table. "Lily is the kindest and prettiest girl around. She is a hard worker and is always thinking up ways to help people out. She can cook and sew and loves the Lord when she remembers she is supposed to put Him first in her life, but she isn't a girl you should fall for. Becky Bates is a much better prospect."

"Oh?" Ben's appetite slackened. "Why do you say that after saying all those fine things about Miss Lily?"

"Because she doesn't want a man who wants to stay in a small town like you do." Great-Aunt Deborah sighed heavily enough to make her body tremble. "Lily was left alone on her family farm for months. Now she wants nothing more than to move to a big city as fast as possible."

Four

Lily shivered, though she felt no cold even in her drafty telegraph office. She experienced the sensation of Ben's hand firm on her arm, and it made her warm all over. A terrible predicament.

"I don't want to find him attractive." She spoke aloud in the empty office. "Mrs. Twining says he wants to stay here, and he works in a livery."

It was a good job. Many ladies would be happy to catch a husband like him. Lily didn't happen to be one of those females who were satisfied with a man who merely had a good job. She didn't need to be rich; she simply wanted to be more than a girl from a farm or a small town.

Now she had even more motivation for wanting to get Ben's room behind the livery fixed up nice so he could move in. Mrs. Willoughby wasn't charging her much rent in exchange for help around the house, and she still took her meals at Mrs. Twining's in exchange for cooking and shopping and housework. Still, even a few bits a week depleted Lily's savings.

"And Mrs. Twining wants him to stay with her." Lily rubbed her eyes.

She had scarcely slept since her encounter with Ben the day before. All night, she'd tossed and turned, remembering, touching her arm, trying to rub away the tingle, trying not to see his face, which looked as dazed as she'd felt.

Good. Maybe he didn't want to like her, either. He needed a nice, quiet girl. Becky would be perfect for him. She wanted nothing more than a home and family and maybe a trip into Davenport for shopping once a year.

Lily shuddered again and took a message off the telegraph regarding a robbery in Des Moines; she would pass it along to the sheriff in case the thieves came to Browning City.

Jake would want the news, too. He was always looking for sensational news for his paper. Today's issue had a long article about Ben Purcell arriving and getting shot. It ended with a plea for someone to confess to the crime or give information about the gunman.

If only the incident had scared Ben off —

Lily interrupted her thought before she finished it. "Please forgive me, Lord. I am being so unkind to him, and he is making Mrs. Twining so happy."

Miserable about her uncharitable attitude toward Ben Purcell, Lily escaped from the telegraph office the minute Toby arrived and said little to Theo as they trotted straight to Becky's house.

"Will you come help me with the livery living quarters?" she greeted her friend.

Becky jumped back and flung up her hands. "Help! I think I've been run over by a locomotive. Where did it come from?"

"I'm only a freight wagon." Lily laughed and dropped her hat and coat onto a chest inside the Bateses' front door.

"Headed downhill. Come have some coffee or something and tell me what this is all about." Becky turned and directed her steps toward the kitchen. "I haven't seen you long enough this week to talk, and you were the first person to meet Ben Purcell."

"Theo met him at the train, but we never had a proper introduction." With the familiarity of many visits, Lily began to take cups and saucers out of the cupboard while Becky set a coffeepot on the stove. "And he was kind of crazy in the head when I first spoke with him. Kept talking about seeing angels."

"Was he that close to death?" Becky turned her face to show her eyes wide with horror. "I thought it was just a scalp wound."

"It was." Lily set down the cups and hugged her friend. "He thought I was an angel is all. Silly man."

"I think that is terribly romantic." Becky sighed. "Do you think it was love at first sight?"

"No such thing." Lily remembered the jolt at his touch on her arm and turned away in case she blushed. "Now, if he'd seen you, I'd believe it."

"Ha. I'm too dark to be mistaken for an angel."

Becky did have dark hair and eyes, and the roses in her cheeks made her complexion glow with good health. In Lily's opinion, Becky was the prettiest girl in Browning City.

"I went to the mercantile today, and Mr. Gilchrist said he would send over all the things we need to make that room behind the livery fine to live in." Lily spoke too fast in her desire to change the subject away from talk of romance and Ben Purcell.

She could talk about Ben Purcell and his

having a nice place to live besides Mrs. Twining's.

"It needs to be cleaned and some rugs put on the floor and curtains and things. But the walls are solid. Will you help me?"

"You know I will." Becky left the coffee simmering and lifted the lid on a pot of rice and beans.

Spicy steam drifted into the room.

"I thought red beans and rice were for Mondays." Lily inhaled the exotic aroma.

Becky's parents were from Louisiana and ate things not common in Browning City.

"It is, but Momma was sick on Monday, so we put off the washing." Becky lowered her voice. "I think she's increasing. Imagine that. Me with another brother or sister when I'm nineteen."

"You're so lucky." Lily's tone was wistful.

She never stopped missing her family.

"We are blessed, but you will be one day, too. God will give you a family again."

Lily said nothing. She wasn't so sure Becky was right.

"Do you want a dish of this rice before the hordes come in to eat it all?" Becky asked.

"I'll wait for the hordes."

Lily enjoyed the tumult around the Bateses' dinner table. She never failed to

61

leave smiling.

"We can talk about how to fix up that room until they come. Mr. Purcell needs a place of his own to live."

Becky nodded. "Especially since everyone says he intends to stay here for good."

Saturday afternoon, Lily and Becky stood in the middle of the living quarters behind the livery barn and grimaced at each other.

"It's gloomy," Becky pronounced.

"It is." Lily glanced from the small, grimy window to the floor littered with crushed leaves, dirt, and she didn't want to guess what else, to the stove so caked with grease it would catch fire if anyone struck a match near it, let alone inside it. "The last man who lived here must have been a vagabond," Lily said.

"Since Mr. Jones sold it to Mr. Gilchrist, no one's lived here for long." Becky hefted a bristle brush from the supplies Mr. Gilchrist had sent over for them to use. "The last man said he didn't like the sounds the place makes."

"How could he work in a livery and not like the sound of horses?"

Lily thought that the best part. Horses were such beautiful creatures, and she liked the sound of them munching hay and grain.

Becky giggled. "He said people walked around in the livery at night. But he never saw anyone, and we know ghosts don't exist."

"Some folk don't take to being alone."

Lily had imagined all sorts of awful things when she was alone on her family farm, before the bank men came to send her away because she couldn't pay the mortgage.

"But a body isn't really alone here." Becky handed Lily a bucket and picked one up herself. "I mean, there are all sorts of people close by, and I don't know a soul here who wouldn't let you in for a talk and cup of coffee."

"Me, either." Lily headed for the pump in the yard. Hot water would be better than the icy stuff that would come out of the well, but she dared not light the stove. "We'll clean that stove first. The rest will be easy after that."

It was. After four hours of hard work that left their hands red, dresses soiled, and hearts satisfied with the labor, Lily and Becky found the stove dried out enough for a fire. They lit it and two lanterns then stood back to survey their handiwork.

"It looks nice now," Becky declared.

"It does. I think he'll be comfortable here."

Yellows and oranges might not be the colors a man would choose, but they brightened the dark wood walls with curtains, rag rugs, and a bedspread provided from Mrs. Twining's attic. With the fire warming up the room and a few kitchen utensils inviting a body to cook a simple meal, the room was habitable.

"It's just not as nice as living at Mrs. Twining's." Lily didn't mean to speak her thoughts aloud, but once they were out, she was glad she had. "I know she wants him to stay."

"But you've lived with her for three years." Becky dropped onto the room's only chair, now cushioned with pillows Lily had sewn between messages at the telegraph office. "It's your room."

"It's Mrs. Twining's room."

"And doesn't living with Mrs. Willoughby cost you money?"

"Not much if I do some work for her." Lily leaned against the door leading from the room to the livery — and it opened behind her.

"Yie!" Lily staggered back. Strong hands caught her by the elbows. Ben's hands. She knew it without glancing up.

And she looked a fright with her hair tied up in a kerchief, her face likely smudged, since Becky's was, and her gown soiled. She cared and wondered why she should. She didn't care what Ben thought of her looks. Now, if Matt walked in . . .

"I beg your pardon." Ben still held her elbows. "I didn't expect . . . this." His voice grew husky. "Did you ladies do all this for me?"

"Mrs. Twining and Mr. Gilchrist provided the supplies." Becky, her cheeks rosier than usual, drew her skirt together over a streak of dirt down the front. "We just provided the elbow grease. I'm Becky Bates, Lily's friend, by the way."

"Pleased to meet you, Miss Bates. And thank you." Ben let go. "I thought — I was expecting . . ." He cleared his throat. "How can I thank you?"

"No thanks necessary." Becky spoke to him, but she stared at Lily.

Lily knew why. She wasn't usually tongue-tied. Between embarrassment over Ben's seeing her so grubby and her guilty conscience, words escaped her.

"I feel like I should do something to repay you," Ben continued.

"Don't, please." Lily scampered to the far side of the room and began to fuss with the fall of a curtain. "It was nothing."

"Not to me." Ben's boot heels clicked on the floorboards. "It's the closest thing to a home I've had since I can remember. And I know you gave up a day off to do this for me."

Lily shrugged. She couldn't say that she had nothing better to do; she did. She had lace to crochet and sew on her dress before church the next day, as Matt should be back from his travels. He would be at church, and she could talk to him during the fellowship time afterward.

"Would that be acceptable to you, too, Miss Lily?"

Ben's speaking her name brought Lily back to the present.

She faced him. "I'm sorry. I was thinking of something else."

Good. That would convince him that her work on his room meant nothing to her.

Except it does.

She gulped. "What did you ask?"

Becky's eyes widened, and her mouth formed an O of confusion.

"I asked if I could take you two ladies to dinner at the hotel as a thank-you for your work." Ben smiled at her in a tightlipped way that told her he was unsure of himself.

She wanted to refuse.

She wanted to cry.

She could do neither.

"You need not thank us," she said.

"But . . ." Becky pressed the back of her hand to her lips.

Lily knew Becky would love to go to dinner at the hotel as a guest, because she worked there on the occasions when it was full, such as for a wedding dinner. If Lily refused, Becky couldn't accept.

"We need to clean up," Lily hedged.

"There's time for that." Ben gave her an encouraging smile.

"It won't take either of us long." Becky's face brightened. "It can't be much later than four o'clock."

"All right, then." Lily made herself smile. "Should we meet you there?"

"No, I'll collect both of you. Miss Becky, where do you live?"

Becky gave him directions to her house. "It's on the far side of town but won't take you a minute to get there."

"Then I'll collect you first. Miss Lily, we will see you about six o'clock if that will do."

"It'll do fine." Lily added quietly, "Thank you. Here's the key Mr. Gilchrist gave me when I offered to clean."

"We'd better hurry." Becky headed for the

outside door.

"Good day." Lily gathered up bristle brushes and buckets.

Ben opened the door for them. "I still can't get over all this work you two did. Now I can move in here, and you can come back and stay in your own room."

Lily nodded. She would be a hypocrite if she said he need not do that. Yet she felt as though that were the right thing to say. So she said nothing as she and Becky departed.

"What's wrong?" Becky posed the question the instant they were out of earshot.

"I feel terrible." Lily glanced over her shoulder.

Ben couldn't see them once they were on the street.

"You should have said something. If you're ill, we shouldn't go to dinner."

"Not that kind of terrible. In here." Lily tapped her chest with a bristle brush handle.

"Why? Using your day off to fix that place up should make you feel good. It is a fine example of service to another."

Lily walked several paces in silence then blurted out, "It wasn't a service. It was completely selfish."

"What are you talking about? You aren't at all selfish. I remember the time we all had the influenza —"

"Stop." Lily waved the brush in the air. "Yes, I know I helped your family. You all welcomed me the minute I moved here and didn't know a soul. What else would I do but repay you for your kindness? But this wasn't a repayment."

"Which makes it all that much more special."

"No, it's not special. I did this for me."

"You, but — oh!" The exclamation emerged as though someone had punched Becky in the middle. "You did it so he will move there, and you can return to Mrs. Twining's and not pay rent anymore, right?"

"Right. And that's wrong. And now he wants to take us out to dinner to thank us. And I don't deserve it." Breathless from her speech, Lily fell silent.

Becky said nothing, either. Their footfalls crunched on gravel, and their breath puffed white in the dusk gray air. Around them, lights winked on in the houses and the aromas of cooking suppers wafted into the evening.

Lily's stomach growled. "I guess dinner will be good. Mrs. Meddler sets a fine table. But I don't deserve it."

"Well, I do." Becky stuck her nose in the air pertly, minced a few steps, then laughed. "You know, Lil, sometimes people do nice things for themselves. Your reason for fixing up the room might not be charitable, but I think he wants to take us to dinner because he's sweet on you."

"Nonsense. He doesn't know me."

But he'd looked as stunned as she'd felt when he first touched her arm.

She shook off the memory. "I think he would be a perfect match for you."

"Now who's talking nonsense?" Becky laughed. "Didn't you see how he couldn't stop looking at you?"

"No, I did not."

She'd had her back to him most of the time.

"Well, it's true. He did. That's why I say he's sweet on you."

"If you're right — and I'm not saying you are — he can have his mind changed." Lily smiled, her spirits lightening at the prospect of playing matchmaker. "It's perfect. You want to be a wife and mother here in Browning City. And he says he wants to stay here. He has an excellent position there at the livery, and — stop laughing. People will come out and stare at us. I am serious."

"I know." Becky wiped her eyes on her sleeve. "That's what's so funny." She sobered. "And a little frightening. You usually make things happen like you want them to."

■ ■ ■ ■

Dinner proved to be a success. Determined now to make a match between Becky and Ben, Lily smiled a great deal and said little unless it was to promote her friend in Ben's eyes. He responded to her sallies with a marked interest in Becky, smiling at her, asking her about her family. He had been to Louisiana not long after the war, about the time Becky's family moved north to Iowa, so they had something to talk about that did not include Lily. When they apologized for not including her, she admitted that she would rather listen and learn.

"You know I want to learn all I can about interesting places," she said.

Her plans worked just fine all the way to Becky's. Then she found herself alone with Ben. They strolled through a night cleared of clouds.

This should be Matt beside me! Lily cried out inside her head.

They could talk of all the places the railroad took a body, all the places it would take a body once it expanded even farther around the country. They could discuss moving away to one of those places where people wanted more excitement than a

71

plowing contest and the spring bazaar, sewing bees and an Easter egg hunt.

"I love the peace here." Ben inhaled a lungful of fresh air. "And everything smells so good."

"Does it?" Lily sniffed. "It smells like snow to me."

"Is that what the freshness is? How right are you about that?"

"I've lived in this state all my life. I know how to read the weather."

"In one state all your life." Ben nodded to a lone man stepping out of the hotel. "What's that like? I mean, was it here in Browning City?"

"No, I lived more north. My family had a farm." Lily hugged her arms across her middle.

"Had?" Ben's tone gently probed.

"We lost it."

She didn't want to talk about her family on such a perfect night, even a perfect night with the wrong man.

"I'm sorry. That must have been rough on you."

"Browning City isn't as lonely as the farm got to be, and I like my work."

"But don't you want land?" Ben tilted his head back. "I want land. I want to stand out in a field and stare at a sky like this without a single light to dim the stars."

"I like lights. I like people and noise. It's just the opposite of being left alone like I was."

"Music?"

"Yes. I mean, I like to listen to it. I'm not talented. What about you?"

"Can't carry a tune in a bucket." He laughed.

Lily joined him in the humor, yet she thought maybe he exaggerated. She could not believe a man with the rich timbre of his speaking voice couldn't sing.

"Becky has a lovely singing voice." Lily spoke one more accolade of her friend.

"Becky is a lovely lady."

Lily skipped around the corner leading to Mrs. Willoughby's house. He liked Becky. Wonderful. He thought she was lovely.

Ben paused at the end of Mrs. Willoughby's front walk. "And so are you, Miss Lily. That simple dinner at the hotel wasn't nearly enough to thank the two of you for the time you took to get my room ready for me. I'll have to do —"

"Nothing, please." Lily's tone held desperation. "I — I wasn't being in the least selfless when I cleaned up that room. I was thinking of myself, not you."

A burden lifted from her heart at the

73

confession.

Except Ben laughed. He threw back his head and let the rolling sound drift to the stars.

Lily faced him, shaking her head. "I just admitted that I am a selfish creature, and you laugh at me."

"I'm sorry. I'm not laughing at you. I am laughing because I am so happy to be around a lady who is so refreshingly honest." He touched her cheek with his fingertips. "Of course you did all that work to get your room back. But, to me, that doesn't at all lessen the importance of having my own place to stay, a place that doesn't roll on wheels. And you did that for me, whatever the reason."

"So —" Lily's mouth felt dry. "So did Becky."

"She sure did, and I'm grateful to her, too."

Good. He wasn't singling Lily out. Still . . . that touch on her cheek . . .

"I must get inside." Lily turned away. "I'm freezing. Enjoy your quarters, and thank you again for dinner."

"See you in church?"

"Of course." Lily dashed up the walk and front stoop.

Inside Mrs. Willoughby's house, which

always smelled of camphor, Lily paused to listen to Ben's retreating footfalls. He had an easy stride that diminished quickly into the distance. A fine man who was all wrong for her. She must continue her efforts to match him up with Becky.

"How do I get them together?"

Church was impossible. Becky sat with her family to help keep her siblings in line. After the service, her mother needed Becky to corral the children into coats and a line to herd them home. No, Lily needed to get Becky away from her family so she would be free to show Ben more of her charm.

Thinking about an opportunity to play matchmaker, Lily slept little that night. The next day, her head swam with rejected ideas and too little sleep until Mary, the pastor's wife, reminded the congregation of the Easter egg hunt coming up in six weeks.

"We will have a separate party for the adults afterward."

No entertainment for six weeks? Too long. Lily would plan a party, a "welcome to Browning City" party for Ben. Mrs. Twining would be in favor of the idea. Best of all, she'd make certain he met everyone in town he should, as well as get to better know his future wife. It was the least she could do to repay him for being so gracious about her selfish motives for fixing up his chamber.

FIVE

"You should come into the parlor and join us." Ben stood in the doorway to the over-heated kitchen and smiled down at Lily. "The kitchen won't fly away if you aren't here to hold it down."

"But the coffee may boil over." Lily picked up a knife. "And if people want more cake —"

"They can come get it themselves. Now come along. You haven't sat down for a minute since the guests arrived." Ben held out his hand to her.

As she did anytime they met, and shaking hands or even giving an object like a plate or cup to one another that might result in his touching her, Lily skittered away like a frightened rabbit. She busied herself with something, even unnecessary tasks, to avoid being near him.

The reaction made Ben smile. If she were indifferent to him, she wouldn't work so hard to keep out of his way.

"Or I could just take the rest of this food into the parlor for you." He started to lift the heavy tray of cake and sandwiches. "Will that do?"

"No, no, I need to keep them covered." Lily flicked a tea towel over the lot. "They'll go stale if I don't keep them moist, and we can't have a towel over them out there. People wouldn't eat anything. So I must stay here and fill plates."

"Everyone here, even my rather infirm great-aunt, can fill his own plate." Ben stepped forward and took Lily's hand.

Despite the heat in the kitchen, her fingers were freezing.

"You need to be near a fire." He glanced at the stove and grinned at her.

That coaxed a slow smile out of her. "Maybe I'm tired."

"But these people are your friends, your neighbors. You've known them for years."

"Only three. They're more your aunt's friends and neighbors. My friends haven't come." She looked so disappointed that he squeezed her hand and gently drew her forward.

"I'm your friend, and I'm here."

"But Becky and Matt aren't, and I particularly wanted them here." She blinked, glanced down, and drew her hand free. "Maybe they'll come later."

"If they do, you'll be closer to the door to greet them."

Lily looked up at him and laughed. "Did you sell things with your father?"

"I did. I was especially good at selling pretty ribbons to the ladies."

"I can imagine you were." She set the last sandwich on the tray. "Now, do you think anyone in the parlor wants anything?"

"Your presence." Ben opened the door again. "At least I do, and I'm the guest of honor. So come along."

"Yes, sir." Lily headed for the doorway, stopped, and yanked off her apron.

Ben decided not to tell her that a loose curl bobbed on the back of her neck. It looked so sweet he wanted to touch it to see if it felt as silky as it looked.

He followed her and the bouncing curl from the kitchen.

In the parlor, a blazing fire and a dozen voices greeted them with warmth. Listening to everyone greet Lily, watching their faces light as she entered the room, Ben wondered how she could say that they were not her friends and neighbors. Every man and woman in the parlor received joy from her arrival in their midst.

So did he. The parlor looked complete with her present, as though someone had restored a missing link to a chain. More like the clasp holding it all together.

"Come sit here, Miss Lily." Jake Doerfel, the newspaperman, shifted to sit on the arm of the sofa and left an empty place on the cushion beside Mrs. Reeves, the pastor's wife.

Lily shook her head. "Ben should sit down. He's the guest of honor."

"My great-nephew is too much a gentleman to sit down and leave you standing." Great-Aunt Deborah thumped her cane on the floor. "You should know that by now, Lily. Now sit so we can get back to talking about Ben with him here instead of behind his back."

"Were you really talking about me behind my back?" Ben crossed the room to perch on the edge of the windowsill beside Great-Aunt Deborah. "What were you saying?"

"That you had the good sense not to keep on leading the life your father led." Great-Aunt Deborah scowled. "It's no way to raise a family."

"Or even find a wife," said Jackson Reeves, the pastor, "so you can raise that family."

"Hold up." Ben held up one hand in a staying gesture, palm forward. "I have to establish myself first."

"And meet the young ladies who aren't taken," Jake put in. "Kind of like Miss Lily here." He poked a pencil-thin finger into her shoulder.

She turned the color of a ripe strawberry.

Ben grinned. "She'll do for a start, but I'm sure Browning City has someone else to give me a choice."

"There's Becky Bates and Emma Kirkpatrick and Eva Gilchrist when she's in town, and . . ." Lily rattled off a list of female names a yard long.

She spoke each name so quickly and precisely that Ben wondered if she had them memorized. Since the night he took her and Becky out to dinner at the hotel, Ben suspected that Lily intended to play matchmaker between Becky and him. With everyone watching them, he couldn't resist teasing her a bit more about giving him a selection of young ladies from which to choose.

"I thought maybe this party was going to be a parade of ladies. I'm so disappointed."

Everyone laughed. Everyone except Lily. She looked hurt. Ben thought her lower lip quivered a bit before she drew it between her teeth and ducked her head.

"I guess I scared them off at church last

week," Ben said, regretting having teased Lily.

"Not from what I heard." Jackson guffawed.

"Nor I." Jake began to sketch in the air. "I think I sold a paper to every single female in Browning City. They wanted that drawing I made of you, Ben. If I had a camera and could have taken a photograph, I could have sold those for ten times the cost of a paper."

Laughter broke out again. With the tables turned on him, Ben joined in. He was glad to see Lily smiling.

"I did invite a few more people." Lily glanced toward the door. "I don't know why they haven't come."

"He'll have a chance to meet everyone as the weather improves." Mary Reeves patted Lily's hand.

"This is quite enough of a crowd for this house for now." Great-Aunt Deborah reached for her cup of coffee. "But you'd better take the leftover cake and pie to the church tomorrow, or we'll both get as round as pumpkins."

"So are you glad you settled here even without a bevy of females lined up?" Mr. Gilchrist asked.

"Quite glad." Ben couldn't stop himself

from glancing in Lily's direction.

She was talking with Jake Doerfel. The newspaperman was amusing her. How pretty she was when she laughed.

"Aye, she is a fine-looking girl." Mr. Gilchrist nodded his head, his white hair catching the lamplight and glowing. "But it makes me weary to watch her. Never sits still. If this town doesn't offer her enough excitement, she stirs it up."

Ben grinned. "I can't imagine this town ever having excitement, which is fine with me."

"Oh no, we've had our share of thrills. Mostly because of the gold."

"Lars, please." Great-Aunt Deborah groaned. "Don't bring up that subject again."

But the others had ceased talking and turned to stare at Lars Gilchrist.

"Now, Deborah, you know it's true about the gold being the most excitement we've had here in years." Mr. Gilchrist nodded his head. "Three times now it's brought us a thrill, first when the thieves rode through —"

"Allegedly rode through," Great-Aunt Deborah interrupted.

"Or stayed, I understand." Jake stood as though intending to give a speech.

"No evidence of that." Jackson Reeves looked as thin-lipped as Great-Aunt Deborah did.

"But we have had government men and young women alike seeking that gold." Mary smiled. "Andrew and Tara Nichols and Constance and Hans Van de Kieft looked. None of them found it, but they found their life mates."

"A much richer haul than gold no one is sure exists." Great-Aunt Deborah sounded positively sharp-tongued.

"I don't know much about it." Despite his aunt's disapproval of the subject, Ben wanted details.

He wanted gold. Gold would buy him land, provide him with permanence — a house, a wife, children — far sooner than would working and saving every penny possible.

"Theo did mention something about it when I arrived," he added.

"Theo talks too much." Great-Aunt Deborah held out her coffee cup. "Lily, may I have some more?"

"Of course." Lily sprang to her feet.

"I'll get it," Ben offered.

Lily fetched the cup. "No, Ben, I'll get it. You stay here and talk with your guests."

"It was stolen from the Union at the end

of the war." Jake shifted his weight from foot to foot. "Taken right out from under the noses of some Pinkertons, or so the story goes. They were identified, and some folk in these parts swore they recognized them from drawings. Some said one of the farmers in these parts was involved. But nothing was ever proved or found, and that farmer skedaddled out of here not too long after."

"How much gold?" Ben persisted.

"Too much for a couple of men on horseback to carry," Great-Aunt Deborah snapped.

"Most folk think Jim Mitchell buried it on his farm," Gilchrist said. "But if he did, don't know why he'd've sold all his equipment to me before he left town."

"Constance and Hans live there now," Mary added. "They've never found a thing, and not for lack of trying."

"But the government is still offering a reward for it," Jake said. "A big reward. So the story must be true at least in part, and getting the reward would be worth the try."

"But how does one try in this vast land?" Ben glanced toward the windows, where darkness and the town curtained millions of acres possibly concealing his key to having everything for which he had yearned and prayed since a child.

I'm going to find it, Lord.

Great-Aunt Deborah would not talk about the gold. Ben tried to get more information out of her after the party, but she gave him the same answer every time. "Concentrate on working hard and seeking the Lord's will for your life."

Ben thought, but refrained from saying, that he saw nothing wrong with God wanting him to find the gold. At least he didn't think seeking it would do any harm.

So Monday, with the horses, mule, and both buggies rented out, he left a sign on the livery door that said he would be back shortly. Mr. Gilchrist had told him he could take breaks during the day, especially if everything was rented or if the weather made business slow. Taking advantage of this generosity, Ben strode down Main Street and entered the newspaper office.

"Not surprised to see you." Jake Doerfel grinned at him. "You seemed mighty interested in that gold. Just getting around to sorting out the old issues."

"Did the previous editor keep back issues?" Ben asked.

"Not very regular, and some are water damaged. You're welcome to look." Jake opened a door behind his paperstrewn desk.

"Wish I could make copies of those pages. I could sell them for ten times what a paper costs and make my fortune."

"Do you think that many people would be interested?"

The instant he asked the question, Ben knew it was foolish. From what he had learned, over the past ten years, two young women had come hundreds of miles to find the gold because they had read of it somewhere.

"I'll see what I can learn." Ben circled the desk and entered the back room.

It smelled of mice and dampness, ink and paper. For several moments, he simply stood and stared at the papers stacked from floor to ceiling. Years' worth. Sometimes several copies from the same week, he realized on closer inspection. It appeared as though no one ever threw out an extra paper. He plucked a stack of papers from the pile Jake indicated. War news of the gold disappearing. He began to hunt through the stacks in search of more information. Dust and mildew rose like swamp gas. He began to sneeze. At the end of the half hour he had allowed himself, however, he knew that two men rode through town, put their horses up at the livery, rode on to Jim Mitchell's farm, then disappeared. Only suspicion and speculation tied the men to the vanished gold, especially when Jim Mitchell sold out and disappeared himself. Other than mentions of Miss Constance Miller and Mrs. Tara Nichols coming to town to seek the gold at two different times after the war, the story vanished from the news. Locating further information about the gold appeared as difficult as discovering the treasure itself.

Extremely dirty and a little discouraged, Ben thanked the newspaperman and strode back to the livery in time to collect one buggy and horse and have a cup of coffee before the rest of the animals came in. Feeding, watering, and rubbing them down took up the rest of the day. By dark, he had finished his work. Weary, he wanted to fix his supper and rest. At the same time, he experienced a restlessness he knew stemmed from his pursuit of information about the stolen gold.

"Perhaps this is wrong, Lord?" He shrugged on his coat.

A brisk walk in the frosty air would do him good. But he didn't know where to go until he heard a train whistle blast its mournful tune across the countryside.

According to the clock in the Scott's Bank window, the train was late. He hoped nothing was wrong. Lily would know if something were.

He turned his feet toward the train station. If nothing else, he could escort her home. She shouldn't be walking through the dark anyway. Of course, she might already be home, but no one could blame a body for trying.

He met Lily halfway between the railway station and town, recognizing her quick, light steps crunching on the frozen gravel.

"Lily?"

She gasped. "Oh, Ben, it's you."

"Who did you expect?" He fell into step beside her.

"No one, but since you got shot . . . I admit it. I am a bit nervous on this road now whenever Theo can't walk me home after dark."

"Then I'm glad I'm here to walk you home." He hesitated. "I'm always glad to walk you home if I can get away on time."

He held his breath, waiting for her response.

"Thank you."

Since he expected a rejection of his offer, her simple thanks felt like a blessing.

"I noticed the train was late." He took the first item of conversation that came to him.

"Nearly half an hour. Toby was late, too.

Toby is almost always late. Some ice on the track slowed the train out of Davenport. The land is low there near the river, and ice is a problem."

"Or for the engineer to have a cup of coffee?" he joked.

She smiled. "Something like that. Speaking of ice, it's getting cold again." She shivered. "I think we're going to get more snow."

"Do you smell it?"

"No."

"Then I say we won't. It's March."

"It's also Iowa." She wrapped her arms around herself. "We can get snow in April."

"Thank you for the warning. I'll keep supplies in as much as I can."

"We always do."

They covered a hundred yards or so without speaking.

Then Lily took an audible breath. "I saw you met all the people at church who didn't come on Saturday."

"Yes, they were all generous enough to introduce themselves and apologize for not attending."

"That was good of them, but I still wish they had been able to come."

"It was only a handful."

"But I like lots of people around." Lily

sighed. "Twelve does not make a respectable number for a party. And it was just too bad that Becky had a cold in her head. And the others had other commitments. Young people, I mean," she finished in a rush.

"Lily, I enjoyed every minute." He wanted to touch her hand, reassure her that the gathering in his honor pleased him more than mere words could express. He would try, though. "I might have had parties when I was a child, but I don't recall. So as far as I am concerned, Saturday was the first one meant for me I've ever had. And that makes it perfect."

"Thank you." In the faint light drifting from the houses, he caught her shy smile slanted in his direction.

His heart contracted. His breath caught in his throat. Great-Aunt Deborah's words came to him, reminding him that Lily wasn't for him. Yet no amount of words could stop a body from caring about another.

He needed to change the subject, make it less personal before he said something that would scare her off. He needed time to convince her to stay — if she was supposed to.

If she was meant for him.

Until he knew one way or the other, he

saw nothing wrong with capturing her attention.

"I thought the discussion of the gold was interesting."

"It was." Lily looked thoughtful for a moment as they approached Great-Aunt Deborah's house.

"Did I say something wrong?" he asked.

"Not wrong . . ." She stepped onto the bottom tread of the porch stairs. "It's a never-ending source of fascination to all of us here in Browning City."

"Except for Great-Aunt Deborah."

"Except for Mrs. Twining." Lily clasped her gloved hands together beneath her chin and gazed at him. "You see, she doesn't like the talk because one of the legends surrounding the gold is that the last place anyone ever saw one of the robbers or his saddlebags was in the livery."

"And her husband, my great-uncle, owned it then."

Six

Lily knew of only one way to divert a man's interest from her — make matters clear to him that her interests lay elsewhere. That was exactly what she must do where Ben was concerned. She knew he liked her more than she wanted him to. So she must show him that she would have a man like Matt Campbell or nobody at all in Browning City.

Matt wouldn't stay in Browning City any longer than she would. His work with the railroad would carry him away as soon as a promotion came his way.

Typing in a message for the Davenport station regarding Matt, Lily thought a promotion was likely to come his way sooner than later. Good for her sake if she could engage his interest in her. She had not yet managed to get herself out of this back of beyond town through promotion. All the city jobs went to operators with more seniority. She would get out through marriage or money.

Money. Strange how Ben wanted to find the gold as much as anyone else did. Lily thought he was above that sort of hankering after wealth. Perhaps he possessed more ambition than she suspected. If only those ambitions didn't still seem to turn toward this outpost of Iowa civilization, she would find his attentions pleasing. Disturbing.

His touch on her cheek the other night had blurred her mind. Such a reaction seemed wrong to her, and she considered discussing it with Mary Reeves. Surely she should not find Ben attractive while setting her sights on another man.

And that other man was on his way home to Browning City. His train would come in too late for Lily to still be at work, but now Becky could include him in the planning committee for the Easter egg hunt. Since his parents' house, where he stayed when in town, lay only a block from Mrs. Twining's, he could walk her over to Becky's house. Lily knew she could get Becky to manage that for her.

So she dressed with care the night of the committee meeting. Nothing too fancy. She didn't have an extensive wardrobe. But she pinned a crocheted collar to her blue wool dress and another fall of lace around the knot of her hair. Pleased that she looked as good as she could, she listened for approaching footfalls and a knock on the door.

She heard whistling first. Tuneless whistling. Odd. Matt never whistled to her knowledge.

At the first *crunch* of a step on the front walk, Lily began to suspect the worst. When the knock sounded, she knew she was right.

With a sinking heart, she opened the door. "Good evening, Ben. You came out of your way to fetch me."

"Only two blocks." He removed his hat and stepped into the entryway. "Good evening, Great-Aunt Deborah. What are you reading?"

"Judges, lad." Mrs. Twining held up her Bible, a finger marking her place between the pages. "What scripture have you read lately, Ben?"

"The Gospel of Matthew." He looked at Lily.

She knew they wanted her to share what she, too, was reading. Except she hadn't read her Bible recently. She had been too busy making lace and working either at the telegraph office or for Mrs. Twining. She was too tired at night and too rushed in the morning.

"I've been neglectful." At least she knew

enough to confess her sin to other Christians.

"You can't know God's will for your life without reading His Word." Mrs. Twining appeared sad rather than reproving.

Lily nodded and turned to pluck her coat from a hook by the door. "I always intend to read it. . . . I know that's not good enough. I'll start tomorrow."

"I'll look in on you." Ben's smile took the sting out of his words, but Lily still felt chastised.

"We should go." She opened the front door. "We can walk over with Matt Campbell. He should be on his way here any minute."

"He's already gone to Becky's house," Ben said. "He carried some things home from the mercantile for her."

"I see."

Lily did see and didn't like the picture. Becky and Matt? No, that wouldn't do at all.

He was probably just being kind.

While neglecting me.

Ben closed the front door behind them. "He asked me to come fetch you."

So he hadn't neglected her. That helped a bit.

But not enough.

"Were you all in the mercantile?" Lily set off at a brisk pace. "Or did he go to the livery to ask you?"

"We were all at the mercantile." Ben's voice held a note of amusement. "He did have to run back to ask me to come by for you, if that helps."

"Helps with what?"

"Your feeling like he forgot about you in favor of Becky."

"I —" Lily's cheeks stung with the flush of embarrassment.

"I expect that's interesting work as a railroad engineer." Ben slipped his hand beneath her elbow. "Takes him all sorts of places."

Lily tensed herself against liking Ben's fingers cupping her arm. "It is. He's interesting. When a body can get him to talk, he'll tell you about all those mountains and cities and lonely plains. . . ." Her voice choked up on her. The lights from the houses blurred before her eyes. Her longing for what seemed impossible to get became a physical ache.

"It's not all good, Lily." Ben's tone was gentle. "It's lonely and cold and wearying to the soul to always be moving."

"Matt doesn't think so."

"Of course he does."

"How do you know? Do you know him as well as I do?"

"Maybe — ah, there are Eva Gilchrist and Tom Bailyn. Now that's an interesting pair, with her daddy owning one mercantile and Tom owning the other."

"I haven't talked to her since she got home." Lily wanted to run up to Eva and bombard her with questions about Philadelphia, but she held back. "She's been visiting her mother's folks."

Eva and Tom waited for Lily and Ben. When a wagon rumbled past, Lily managed to fall into step beside Eva, forcing the men behind them.

"I can't wait to see what you're wearing. Is it very smart and new?"

"Of course." Eva let out her low chuckle of a laugh. "And yes, I will be happy to let you copy the pattern. But it does feel good to be home. I am fatigued to death with all the social calls they arranged for me while trying to find me a husband."

"Did they succeed?" Lily tried to think how to extract every detail of Eva's journey from her. "Are you engaged?"

"No. None of them had any intention of coming west to take over Daddy's business or the farm with me."

"With —" Lily stopped so abruptly, Ben

stepped on the back of her heel.

"I beg your pardon," he apologized.

"My fault." Lily wriggled her heel back into her shoe. "I was just so surprised I forgot to keep walking. Eva, you didn't really want to come back here, did you?"

"I did." Eva linked her arm with Lily's and got the party moving again. "I love Iowa in the spring. And I missed church. My relatives hardly ever go."

The instant they reached the bottom of the front walk to Becky's house, four children burst from the front door and raced out to surround them with excited chatter regarding their likes and dislikes for the Easter egg hunt.

"Did you say you want a real chicken instead of an egg?" Lily scooped up the youngest child and carried her to the house. "That could be kind of hard to catch."

"I'd do it." Molly, a four-year-old cherub in looks and imp in behavior, hooked her arm around Lily's neck. " 'Cause then we would always have eggs to bake cakes."

"Ah, is that why?" Smiling, Lily entered the warmth of the Bateses' house.

Several minutes of confusion reigned while Mrs. Bates hustled the children off to bed, Mr. Bates collected coats and hats, and

Becky asked people's preference for coffee or tea.

Lily loved every minute of the hubbub. She wished it would continue or that she lived in a household like Becky's — one that rarely knew peace and quiet. She knew she would be alone in the city if she didn't have a husband with whom she could move there, but she believed she would never feel alone with hundreds of people within shouting distance.

At last, the six of them sat around the Bateses' kitchen table, and Matt lifted a sheet of foolscap off the top of a block of writing paper. "Becky and I already made a list of things we need to accomplish." He flashed his wide grin at her. "She was just full of ideas. Good ones."

Becky blushed and grinned back.

Lily stared. Coffee burned in her stomach.

She must be mistaken. Surely Matt and Becky weren't courting. Surely he would find her dull.

But how could anyone find Becky dull? She was lively and pretty and smart. Lily adored her. That Matt adored her, too, seemed inevitable.

But I wanted Ben to fall for her.

Ben scarcely noted Becky's presence. He danced attendance on Eva and Lily, leaving

Matt to fetch and carry anything Becky needed and Tom to crack jokes about having nothing to do and putting his feet up.

Lily admitted — grudgingly — that Becky and Matt looked good together. They both had fine, dark eyes and curly dark hair. They both shared brilliant, white smiles.

But they didn't share anything else. Lily knew it. Becky wanted to stay put. Matt traveled. Becky would never like that.

Lord, can't they see that this will be disastrous for them?

Lily was so engrossed in her concerns that she didn't notice the conversation turning away from the Easter egg hunt party to a charitable event to start a library in Browning City — due to Eva's sojourn to the East.

"I did enjoy going," she said. "I enjoy coming home even more."

"I feel the same way." Matt nodded. "When I see the Browning City depot coming into view, I want to pile on steam and get here faster."

"You don't want to shoot out of here faster?" Lily asked before she could stop herself.

"Not any faster than necessary." Matt picked up his coffee cup and held it between his hands. A dreamy expression came over his face. "I pass farm after farm with each trip, and I can't help but wonder what it would be like to stay put year after year."

"Tedious," Lily murmured.

"Traveling is tedious." Ben looked straight at her, though he addressed the group. "I did it for nearly twenty years. When I gave my heart to the Lord, the first thing He had to work on with me was not envying all those folks I passed who had real houses to live in."

"A real house is good." Lily agreed with him on that. "We had a snug one on our family farm. But it went the same way as the land — to the bank. So a body may as well not have one."

"Unless you can pay for it outright," Tom put in. "I waited to buy the mercantile from Evan Cooper until I could own it outright and have living quarters above."

"I intend to do the same thing," Ben said. "I may be old and gray before I can afford a farm, but I'll own it."

"I just worked out today that I can buy the farm I want." Matt made the announcement in a quiet voice that rang with joy.

And he gazed at Becky when he said it.

Lily stared at him. "You are giving up the railroad? Travel? All those places you talk about?"

"Yes, ma'am, I am." Matt looked like he would burst with joy. "I turned in my notice today."

"But just the other day . . ." Lily stopped. She couldn't say what the telegram about him contained, the praise for his skill and recommendation for promotion to more regular routes. But if he knew, surely he would change his mind.

"I was offered a better position." Matt spoke as though reading her mind. "You probably knew that, Lily."

She nodded.

"I'd have been traveling between Des Moines and Chicago and home regularly. More pay, too. But I turned it down. I'm thirty-two. It's time I settled down."

Lily felt as though someone had yanked a chair out from beneath her. If she were able to find work elsewhere, especially work with more pay, she wouldn't turn it down. For months, she had pinned her hopes of getting out of Browning City on her savings growing and on Matt Campbell taking a serious interest in combining their futures at the altar. Now all she could count on were her savings, and they looked too pitiful for any kind of life in the city. Yet she counted herself fortunate that he had fallen for Becky instead of her.

"Lily?" Ben laid his hand on the back of her chair. "You look a bit peaked. Do you want to go home?"

She did feel unwell.

"Yes, please." She gave everyone a bright smile. "Good night, everyone. May I call on you Sunday afternoon to look at your Eastern clothes, Eva?"

"Right after church. Come to dinner." Eva kissed Lily's cheek. "It'll be fun because I am going to get a lace collar out of you yet."

Lily said her good-byes to the others and allowed Ben to usher her from the house.

Neither of them spoke for the first three blocks. Around them, the night lay still save for the hiss of wind through bare tree branches and a banging shutter somewhere in the distance. Clouds obscured the sky, and though they didn't have a lantern to brighten the streets, Lily knew every hollow and rut well enough not to trip in the poor light as long as she concentrated. If Ben remained silent, she could pay attention to her feet.

"Why do you think the city is so grand?" He broke the stillness with a question that made Lily stumble.

She set her chin. "It has more people and more lights and more things going on. A body doesn't get lonely there."

"You're mistaken in that, Lily." He took her gloved hand in his. "I was lonely all the time when I was in the city."

"You were lonely all the time you were traveling, from what you said."

She knew she should withdraw her hand from his, but she liked the strength of his fingers around hers.

"I was until I met the Lord face-to-face, so to speak." His voice held a smile. "I talked to Him after that whenever Pa didn't have much to say. He didn't have much to say very often unless he was selling one of his goods from the wagon. He sure could make friends then."

"He must have met a trainload of people over the years." Lily knew she sounded wistful as she gazed into the distance. "Lots of people to be friends with at any time."

"Lily." Ben stopped and faced her. "When my father died, not one person he had met over the years was there. He collapsed in the street in Chicago, and not one person came to his aid."

"That's . . . terrible." Lily shook her head to clear it. "I mean, you'd think someone would stop."

"You would." Ben tightened his hand on hers. "I found him myself about the time a policeman got there."

"So someone did summon help." Lily felt relief lightening her mood.

"Someone complained about him blocking their shop doorway."

Lily flinched. "That must have hurt you terribly."

"You know what hurt worse?" Ben resumed walking, urging Lily along with him. "No one came to his funeral. I sent notices to the paper. I thought a few of his regular customers would come or a few people he'd helped along the way would take a minute to pay their respects. But no one did."

"I'm so sorry. But if he had stayed in that one place for years, it would have been different."

"Possibly for the funeral, yes, but not the other. No one can live in a city long enough to know everybody."

"But that's part of what must be interesting about it. I mean, someone new is always around the corner, unlike here." Lily waved her hand to the silent, near-dark town. "Other than Jake Doerfel buying the old newspaper last month, you were the first person to come here to stay permanently in an age."

"And you and Theo stopped to help this stranger."

"We knew who you were. Of course we

helped Mrs. Twining's great-nephew."

"And you helped me because you both knew her."

Lily wanted to argue with him, but words escaped her until they reached Mrs. Twining's street.

"Ben, life isn't all good in a small town. We have people here, and that means we have bad things happen. People get into fights and steal things. Someone stole my pocketbook right out of the telegraph office one day. I'd just gotten paid and didn't have time to get to the bank. When I ran out to give a message to Theo to deliver, my money vanished."

"That must have been rough on you."

"More than rough. I had to eat into my savings to get by until my next pay. And I'm not a stranger here. I've lived in Browning City for three years. Everyone knows me because of the telegraph."

"I think everyone knows you because of everything you do here."

"Which is just what I'm saying." Lily yanked her hand from his at last and curled her fingers into fists. "I am always organizing one function or another to make this town more entertaining, and I find ways to raise money for the school and church . . . and then someone steals from me."

"Could it have been someone from the train and not a Browning City resident at all?"

"It . . ." Lily thought a moment. "I suppose it could have been."

"And maybe they really needed that money. I'm not saying their action was right, but considering that money as a gift to the Lord instead of something taken from you helps."

Lily took in his words and nodded. "It does. Ben, I . . ." She gazed up at him and wished she could see his face clearly. "I truly admire your faith in God. I could never have thought of things that way."

He chuckled. "It's easy to give others advice. I'd probably feel about the same as you if someone stole my pay."

"Just put it in the bank immediately. The bankers are trustworthy here."

"I know, but they're both customers, so I don't know which one to use."

"Half to each?"

They laughed as they headed onto the porch.

Lily rested her hand on the doorknob. "Good night, Ben. Thank you."

Ben brushed the knuckles of his gloved hand across her cheekbone. "Thank you, Lily."

Before she could ask him for what he'd thanked her, he turned and strode down the walk to the street.

Lily slipped inside and locked the door behind her. But that was as far as she moved toward readying herself for sleep. Instead, she leaned against the door and listened to his footfalls dwindle into the distance.

When she no longer heard him, she tilted her face to heaven. "I know now that I am a poor Christian, Lord. I don't know what to do about it yet, but I have a feeling I'm going to find out."

She suspected that Ben would continue to play a role in showing her. Such a pity he wasn't the right man to play a far different role in her life.

Seven

No matter how many times Ben examined the livery, he could not figure out how anyone could have hidden so much as a half eagle in the building, let alone an entire cache of stolen gold. Walls, floor, and roof consisted of boards fitted together with near seamless perfection. When his great-uncle built the livery, he'd constructed it to last through generations of Iowa winds and weather. Even Ben's little room in the back demonstrated craftsmanship meant for longevity. If legend of the thieves having cached their illicit loot in the livery bore any fragment of truth, someone far more clever than Ben would have to work out how they'd accomplished the task.

He thought perhaps the thieves stowed it amid a collection of farm equipment gathering dust in one corner of the building. Mr. Gilchrist had said that soon after purchasing the livery he'd bought the equipment from Jim Mitchell, a farmer leaving the district. It was of little to no interest to Ben, so he turned his attention to the hayloft, but only briefly. One look around told him that nothing stashed up there would go unnoticed for months, let alone years.

No, the gold was not in the livery any more than it had been in any other locations treasure hunters had explored over the eleven years since the war ended and the money disappeared. He had no more chance of finding easy wealth than had anyone else.

Disappointment lay heavy on his heart. He didn't long for a quick addition to his savings because he was lazy. He liked exerting himself, found great satisfaction in ending a day with the knowledge that he had wasted few to no minutes of his time. He liked the sensation of muscles fatigued from honest labor rather than aching from sitting still.

But he wanted to remain in Browning City. He had been here a month and knew he had found the place he had sought since growing old enough to realize that life on the road was not what most other folks experienced in their lives. Browning City was home. Perhaps he recalled something of the place from his childhood, though Great-Aunt Deborah pointed out how much the town had changed in twenty years. Two banks. Two general stores. A newspaper. Farmers had come and gone, prospered and failed, grown restless and settled down to build the next generation.

Ben wanted to settle down and build the next generation — with Lily at his side.

Except Lily didn't want to be at his side. She yearned for life beyond the rolling prairies of Iowa. She sought the faster pace of the city because it was as far from her homeland as a body could imagine.

Having spent much of his life moving from farmland to small town, from village to metropolis, Ben knew happiness did not lie in crowds and one entertainment after another. The pleasure was fleeting, leaving one emptier afterward than before. He suspected that Lily would learn this for herself once she had the experience. He feared she would suffer for insisting that she learned.

He didn't want her to suffer. Lily Reese had seen too much pain in her life already. Ben wanted to give her joy, make her laugh, meet life's challenges together.

"Thy will be done, Lord." He meant what he said at the end of each prayer for his future. Yet at the same time, visions of a reward for locating government gold glittered in the corners of his mind.

With gold, he could have his own land while he was still young enough to work it hard and make it prosper. He could do more. He could provide his wife with occasional journeys to Chicago, enough so she would appreciate the camaraderie and caring of a small town.

Without the miracle of finding gold, Ben resigned himself to waiting while he saved enough from his wages to purchase land and observing Lily's search for happiness in ceaseless activity.

Lily was involved in so many different activities Ben couldn't keep them all straight. Easter egg hunt for the children. Easter egg hunt and party for adults. Something she called the spring bazaar. Each planning meeting and preparation seemed to take up her time to the exclusion of walking with him. She didn't even stay in the parlor and visit when he called on Great-Aunt Deborah. After serving them coffee and cake or cookies, she escaped into the kitchen, her room, or to someone else's home.

Ben suspected she was avoiding him.

The idea of that made him smile. She had to have some kind of feelings for him to make herself scarce whenever he was around.

As March slipped into its latter half, Ben grew weary of fleeting glimpses of Lily and even more rare conversations, despite their paths crossing during church and at the homes of mutual acquaintances. He took matters into his own hands. On a day warm enough to promise spring in the near future, in spite of heavy rainfall, a day too wet for anyone to be interested in riding, Ben took out one of the buggies and drove it toward the train station. All the way, riding with the top up, he scanned the road for a diminutive figure trudging through the mud.

He caught up with her halfway between railroad and town.

"Climb in." He reined in beside her. "You're drenched."

She glanced up, and a stream of rain cascaded into her face. She wiped it away with a soaked sleeve. "Is something wrong? Mrs. Twining?"

"No, nothing's wrong."

She crossed her arms over her middle. "Then why are you here?"

"It's raining. Business was slow at the livery." He grinned at her. "I thought I could offer a pretty lady a ride under those circumstances."

"You can. . . ." She laughed. "You know I can't say no." She took his hand, gathered up her skirt, and swung herself aboard. "I think you're taking advantage of me, Mr. Purcell."

"Mr. Purcell?" He handed her a dry rug to place over her knees before getting the horse going again. "I know you've been a stranger lately, but surely not that much."

"I apologize." She settled back against the seat while he turned the buggy back toward Browning City. "Some inspectors from Western Union were here all day, so I've been calling everyone, even Theo, 'Mister.' "

"Is something wrong at the telegraph office?"

Ben's gut tightened. If the company discontinued Browning City's telegraph service, Lily would leave before he had a chance to change her mind about the town. Worse, it would confirm her belief that Browning City was too much of a backwater to endure any longer.

"I think all is well." Lily tucked her hands inside her coat sleeves. "They were nice to me, but they wanted to see how fast I can key in a message."

"Are you fast?"

"Compared to the other operators, yes, but I don't know about the ones in the city offices where they get more messages."

"Do you want to be faster than they are?" He held the horse to a slow, steady pace to make the drive last a handful of minutes longer.

"I like to be good at what I do." She shifted on the seat so she faced him. "If nothing is wrong, why did you come fetch me?"

"It's raining. And" — he gripped the reins — "I wanted a chance to see you."

"Why?"

"I never get to see you anymore."

She drew her golden brows together. "I saw you at church yesterday."

"Saw me, yes. But you didn't speak to me."

"No, I didn't." She repositioned herself to face the curtain of rain sluicing off the buggy top in a silvery curtain. "We're fortunate this isn't snow."

"And maybe you count yourself fortunate that this drive is so short." He spoke more harshly than he intended but didn't regret doing so.

He couldn't stop her from evading him in the street or at church, but she didn't need to switch the subject to the weather, something strangers might discuss in a railroad car, while riding in a buggy with him.

He tightened his hands on the reins and sent the horse careening around the last corner faster than prudent. A wheel slipped in the muddy street, and the buggy lurched.

Lily grasped the edge of the seat. "You're angry with me."

"I am annoyed." He slowed the vehicle to a halt before Great-Aunt Deborah's house. "I want to know what happened to the lady who was honest enough to admit she helped me out of selfishness."

"You want me to admit to some other wrong to you? Because I won't." She glared up at him for a moment then turned away. "I haven't done anything bad to you. I simply have other responsibilities and interests that don't include you."

"Is that the truth?"

She continued to gaze into the wet darkness.

"At least you aren't telling more than one lie."

She stiffened. "I never lied."

"You exaggerate the truth, then."

"I — maybe a little." Her tone held the tiniest hint of a laugh.

"Much better." He lifted a strand of damp hair from where it clung to her cheek. "May I ask why — in a warmer place than here?"

"Mrs. Twining has her ladies' prayer meeting tonight. I usually attend, but if you insist, I guess you can come into the kitchen."

"Don't sound so unhappy about the prospect of my calling."

"I don't want you to call." She flicked the rug aside, rose, and stepped down from the buggy without assistance. "I'm just being polite in letting you come by for coffee."

"Thank you." He tipped his hat. "I'll be there at seven o'clock."

"Seven thirty."

"Yes, ma'am."

He watched her until she disappeared into the house; then he drove around to the livery. Horse and buggy dried as best as he could, and the former fed, he entered his quarters to prepare his simple meal of bread, cheese, and a rather withered apple from the previous year's harvest. The two hours he had to wait dragged so long he took up one of the books that had gone with his father and him around the country. It was one of his mother's books, something more appealing to females, he supposed, so he'd never read it. But, while waiting until he could see Lily, he grew so engrossed in the tale of a young woman and her foolish choices he realized he was going to be late.

He dropped the book onto the table and

jumped up from the chair so fast he knocked it over. Leaving it where it lay, he snatched his coat from its hook by the door and dashed into the night. Remembering he forgot to lock the door, he turned back, locked up, and sprinted through the rain.

At Great-Aunt Deborah's house, he saw the shadows of several ladies through the lace curtains, so he circled the house to the back door.

Lily opened it before he raised his hand to knock. "You're soaked, and the temperature is dropping. Come in and get warm by the fire."

He gazed at Lily, her hair tied back with a ribbon, her gown a faded calico, and felt warmed already.

"You look really pretty," he blurted out before he could stop himself.

"I look like a schoolgirl, but my hair was wet."

"You look like a pretty lady to me." He clasped his hands behind his back. "But you don't want compliments from me."

"I —" She compressed her lips. Then she raised her head and met his look with a twinkle in her eyes. "You already caught me nearly telling a fib tonight. I won't tell another one by saying I don't like compliments as much as the next female. But I will say that I'd rather you didn't give them to me."

"Why not?"

"I'm not staying here." She turned toward the stove and picked up the coffeepot. "I'd best make more with those ladies out there."

Without asking her, Ben began to take cups and saucers from the cupboard and set them on the table. He found spoons and set them beside the cups in perfect alignment with the coffee things. Did he have the correct side? Somewhere he had heard or read about a proper way to set things out. He didn't recall what the procedure was. He simply concentrated on each detail until he knew he could make his tone casual when he asked, "When?"

"I have no idea." She dipped water into the coffeepot.

"Maybe as soon as May, after the plowing contest."

"After the what?"

"A plowing contest. We have it every year at the same time as the spring bazaar."

Something niggled at his mind.

"That's right. Theo mentioned it my first day here, I think." He drew out a chair. "Why don't you tell me about it while the coffee boils?"

"It's just what it sounds like." She took

the proffered seat.

"Men from all over come. They pay a small fee; then they take a plow and see who can plow the straightest and fastest furrow down a field. It's a cash prize."

"So it's a race while drawing a plow." He took a chair facing her. "Or does one get to use a horse or mule?"

"No, you pull it yourself." She picked up the spoon from beside her saucer, moving it about in circles against the pine surface. "It's a comfortable prize."

"A pity I don't have a plow. I have spent many springs plowing fields. My father and I hired ourselves out when money got tight. I got pretty good at it."

"I think it's a pity ladies aren't allowed to enter." She popped out of her chair and headed for the fragrant-smelling coffee. "I helped plow every year, too. Helped drive the mule until I was seventeen."

"Was that how old you were when your family lost the farm?" He posed the question in a soft voice.

She shook her head. "That was the year I lost my family. A fever came through, and they all died. Typhoid. It didn't kill me, but I was too sick to work. So I lost the farm the next year."

"Lily . . ." He started to rise.

She waved him back down. "I'll go fill up the ladies' cups and come right back." She vanished through the kitchen doorway.

Ben still saw her in his mind's eye, a slight figure. Too slight to have worked behind a plow. Too delicate for year after year of battering Iowa wind and rain, snow and sun. Maybe she was made for town life, not the life of a farmer's wife. Who was he to say she should want a different life from the one she wanted?

That hidden treasure sure could give her an easier life.

Winning the prize for the plowing contest seemed more likely a means of gaining extra money.

If he had a plow.

He was thinking of how he could borrow one from the farm equipment in the livery, when Lily returned and filled his cup without asking and reseated herself across from him.

"I think you want to talk to me about something." She avoided his gaze.

"I want to know why you're too busy to talk to me." He gave her an encouraging smile. She began to make circles with the spoon again. "It's too embarrassing to say."

"May I guess?" She shrugged.

"You don't like me, but because I'm Deborah Twining's great-nephew, you don't want to say so."

She wrinkled her nose. "You know that's not it."

"You don't have time for one more friend."

"No one should be that busy."

"Hmm." He tapped a finger against his chin and stared past her shoulder. "You don't dislike me, and you like lots of friends, so–o–o . . ." He shifted his position and caught her gaze too fast for her to look away. "Maybe you think I like you too much, and you don't want me to."

"I — maybe — yes."

And she liked him too much. He read it in the way she tore her gaze from his and darted her glance around the room. Panic. Afraid he would confront her with that, too.

"I'll let it go at that, Lily." He rose, his coffee untouched.

"But I'm praying for you and for myself, and I'd like you to give me a chance. Please. At least stop avoiding me when we're in the same room together. Agreed? It's just plain hurtful."

That was unfair. Ben suspected Lily couldn't hurt anyone intentionally.

She rose and held out her hand. "I promise to talk to you when our paths cross. But,

Ben, please don't let that happen too often."

"It'll happen as often as the Lord is willing." Grinning, he took her hand, squeezed it, and slipped out the back door.

He whistled all the way to the livery. A man just had to whistle when he knew the lady fast taking hold of his heart wasn't indifferent to him.

Still whistling, he entered the livery through the front door and began his nightly rounds of the horses and mule. He passed by the corner with the discarded farm equipment, an area that should be cleaned out to make room for parking at least one buggy inside. He pulled back the tarpaulin and stared at the things with growing excitement.

The plow was a fine one.

Since the night wasn't far advanced, Ben sprinted across town to Mr. Gilchrist's house. He went to the back door in case the owner was occupied with guests.

Mr. Gilchrist himself stood at the kitchen stove making pancakes. "Come on in, lad. Hungry?"

"I wasn't."

"You are now. Sit down and tell me what brings you out in the rain. Nothing serious, I trust."

"No, sir. Everything is good, though business was slow today."

"Sure, it would be. Sit down. Sit down."

With only a little reluctance to have his boss serve him, Ben sat. Over the hotcakes, he explained about the contest and wanting to borrow the plow.

"I can practice on days off if the weather ever turns nice. If you say it's all right for me to use that old plow in the livery."

"Use it? Lad, you can have it. I have no use for it. No one has ever wanted to rent it."

"Well, thank you, sir. That's very generous, but not necessary."

"Sure it is. I wasn't making any money on that livery until you came along. You keep it making money, and I'll be generous."

As pleased as Ben was to have the plow given to him, he also recognized the gentle threat in Mr. Gilchrist's words — if the livery had a bad month or so, Ben could be out of work.

But the Lord just wouldn't hold up Ben's life like that, not for something so silly and unlikely.

Concern tossed aside, he trotted home through rain that was growing to feel more like ice than water and slipped the key into the lock of his quarters.

The key didn't need to turn.
The door had already been unlocked.

EIGHT

The sound of the closing back door echoing in her ears, Lily propped her elbows on the table and covered her face with her hands. "Lord, I need to leave here. I need to leave here soon."

She needed to leave before she fell in love with Ben Purcell.

If it wasn't already too late.

She shivered despite the warmth of the stove behind her. She couldn't be in love with Ben. It was the most ridiculous notion she had ever had. He wasn't right for her, with his desire to stay put in this small, poky town, where even hat styles were a year or more out-of-date.

Yet not so long ago — so short a time ago, she blushed to remember — she'd thought Matt Campbell was right for her. Maybe she simply knew nothing about love.

That was it. She wasn't falling for Ben Purcell. She just didn't understand what

127

her heart wanted — except to leave Browning City.

The spring bazaar was her biggest hope for earning enough money to seek her fortune in the city. She and some of her friends had rented a booth. Lily intended to sell her handmade lace, the art of which she had learned from her French grandmother. Becky, Eva, and some others intended to sell sweets they made themselves. Lily figured the combination of lace and candy went well together because the children would pull their mothers over to the booth to purchase the treats and the mothers would buy pieces of the lace. On Saturday, they all intended to get together to begin planning how they would decorate the booth and to pore over sweets recipes, possibly even experiment with a few, like the toffee.

They would meet if the weather cooperated. She'd learned never to count on Iowa weather to behave in March. One could have sunshine and blue skies one day and be planning a picnic. The next, a foot of snow might fall and all activity would come to a halt.

Listening to the *tap, tap, tap* of rain against the kitchen window, Lily considered the other offering of an Iowa March — ice.

128

She rose from the table and slipped into the parlor. "Ladies, I'm sorry to interrupt, but it sounds as though the rain has turned to sleet."

Groans met her announcement.

"If any of you wishes, I can walk you home."

"No, no."

"You can't do that and come back by yourself."

"You're too little to support a woman my size."

Protest rained as thick as the ice crystals outside. Ignoring the objections, Lily retrieved her coat and hat and returned to the parlor.

"Take my walking cane, child." Mrs. Twining held it out to her. "It'll give you balance if the streets are slippery."

"Thank you, ma'am, but what will you do?"

"Sit here and stay warm." Mrs. Twining smiled. "And pray you all safely to your doors."

None of the ladies lived far away. Glancing over the three of them, Lily chose the frailest appearing of them and offered her arm. She doubted she could hold the other two up if they fell, but at least she would be there to fetch help.

With much laughter and some genteel shrieks when a foot slipped, the ladies headed through the night. Within a quarter hour, Lily delivered each safely to her door then returned home. Already a glaze of ice coated the wooden front steps. Leaning heavily on Mrs. Twining's cane, Lily reached the door without incident and stepped into the warmth of the house with a prayer of thanksgiving.

"It's treacherous out there." She returned the cane to Mrs. Twining. "But at least this time of year, we know it won't last."

Except it did last. In the morning, Lily woke to an eerie stillness punctuated by the occasional *crack* of a branch breaking under its load of frozen water. She wondered how she would get to work across the slick landscape. Knowing that doing so would take more time than usual, she hurried to dress and prepare a small breakfast.

She was setting a tray of coffee and toast out to carry into Mrs. Twining when someone pounded on the back door.

"Miss Lily?" Toby stood on the other side of the door, shivering. "The lines are down. There aren't any messages getting through in either direction."

"So should I go into the office or not?" Lily backed away from the door so Toby could step into the kitchen.

"No, ma'am. Theo says to stay home." Toby glanced at the coffeepot. "May I —"

"Of course. Let me deliver this tray to Mrs. Twining first."

And take a few minutes to compose myself.

She wanted to cry. At least one day of missed wages. If damage to the wires was bad enough, she would miss more than one day of work.

Once again, she calculated her savings flagging.

She also saw days of boredom ahead. Going anywhere just wasn't safe with inches of ice coating the roads. Broken tree branches fell and struck people down. Wagons lost traction and careened into walkways. Feet slipped out from beneath a body, and the fall broke even the sturdiest legs.

She had to stay home and resign herself to no one calling.

When snow began to fall at noon, she accepted yet more time off work and confinement to the house with Mrs. Twining.

Not that Mrs. Twining was poor company. Lily never tired of hearing the older woman's tales of her early years as a society miss in Philadelphia, how she had fallen for adventurous Mr. Twining and how they had begun their trek west.

"We headed to Michigan first. Then things got too crowded around Detroit, so we moved down into southern Illinois. But Iowa was getting civilized enough for folks to settle and prosper, so we acquired land here and finished raising our children."

"My family did much the same." Lily slipped her hook through a loop of fine, white thread. "But you must have wanted people closer together. I mean, you helped found Browning City."

"We hoped to make this a stage stop so we didn't have to travel so far for goods. It worked, and now we have the train depot and a telegraph."

"But you chose to live in town after it was built up a bit."

"Yes, we did. After our son . . ." Mrs. Twining swallowed. "After our son died, we couldn't keep up with the farm, so we moved into town and bought the livery from the sale of the land."

"I'm sorry you had to give up your homestead." Lily bent over her lace making. "But I'm glad you're here."

"I am, too." Mrs. Twining's voice held a gentle smile. "I wouldn't have your company if we hadn't. Shall I read some scripture to you while you work?"

"Please."

Lily thought about her declaration to Mrs. Twining and Ben weeks ago about reading her Bible more. She hadn't done it much. She knew too many of the verses she might run across, things like not storing up riches and not worrying about the future. So easy for persons who knew what their lives would be to claim that was right. But since her family died, her life had felt unsettled, temporary, poised for the next leap to somewhere else.

She feared Mrs. Twining might choose one of those passages. Instead, she read from the Psalms, chapters of rejoicing in the Lord's love and goodness.

The afternoon wore on. Snowflakes the size of two-bit pieces fell from the sky in an endless barrage. At dusk, the wind kicked up, drifting the snow against trees, fences, and the back door.

Lily had to push with all her strength to open the door so she could fetch more firewood. Wind caught her hat and sent it sailing into the darkness then tore her hair from its pins and flung it across her face in heavy, wet strands.

"I hate this place!" She cried the words into the night, where she knew no one could hear her. "I want to run away."

The kitchen door slammed behind her.

She staggered to the woodpile and grabbed up as many logs as she could hold. Fighting the wind like a beast caught in a locomotive's cowcatcher, she stumbled back to the door and reached for the handle with near-frozen fingers.

Another hand reached it first.

"Let me help you," Ben Purcell shouted over the blizzard's roar.

He opened the door. She toppled inside, dropping logs and gasping for breath. A moment later, he entered with more logs and his own bare head white with snow.

She wanted to hug him. She hadn't felt like hugging a man ever in her life. But the sight of Ben, tall and broad shouldered, sturdy and full of life, sent such a wave of joy through her that she knew she should run as fast and as far away from him as she could.

Except she couldn't run anywhere. The weather held her captive.

Ben's gaze held her captive.

"You — you shouldn't have come out in this," she said through a dry throat.

"I couldn't leave you ladies on your own once the storm grew worse." He set his load of logs in the wood box and stooped to gather up the ones she had dropped. "I think if I hadn't come along, you'd be in

Kansas by now."

"Missouri."

"Hmm?"

"The wind is from the north. It would send me to Missouri."

"Right." He laughed up at her.

Lily wrapped her arms around herself. She fell the rest of the way in love with Ben Purcell.

She couldn't fall out of love with him while he stayed around for the rest of the storm.

"You ladies need someone to fetch and carry for you. It's too bad for either of you to go outside." He made his pronouncement with such authority that even his great-aunt didn't argue with him.

So he fixed himself a pallet on the kitchen floor and kept the stove supplied with wood. When Mrs. Twining and Lily woke the following morning, they found the house warm and breakfast nearly ready.

"Whatever your father did wrong in dragging you around the country," Mrs. Twining told Ben, "he did right when he taught you your manners."

"He said Momma would want me to have them." Ben smiled. " 'Never disrespect a lady of any age or station' was what he told me from the time I was small."

"How is the weather?" Lily changed the subject with an abruptness she knew was rude. She had to. She couldn't tolerate an image of Ben as a small boy with curly dark hair that would forever be unruly and blue eyes that sparkled with mischief. The picture reminded her of children, marriage, life stranded in Iowa because her heart proved to be a foolish instrument.

"The snow is letting up, and the wind has died." Ben studied her face. "Do you need to get to the station?"

"Not if the lines are still down." She stood and began to gather the dishes. "Perhaps we should go out and see if anyone needs help."

Anything not to be confined in the same house with him.

"I did that all day yesterday." Ben lifted a pan of water to heat for dish washing. "Mrs. Willoughby, Miss Hansen, and Mrs. Longerbeam all have plenty of wood and supplies. I believe the others all have family, so I'm here to take care of mine."

"I'm not . . ." Lily stopped herself.

"Of course you're family." Mrs. Twining caught hold of Lily's hand as she reached for an empty coffee cup.

"Thank you." Lily didn't want to hurt the older woman by denying the truth of her words. "I'd better be a good girl and do my chores."

"I'll help." Ben picked up a tea towel.

While Mrs. Twining read to them, they washed up the breakfast dishes. After they finished with that, he insisted on helping Lily with peeling potatoes and carrots for a stew and kneading the bread dough. He brought in more wood, swept the floor, and always stayed far too close to her.

If I don't get away, Lord, Lily prayed when she managed a few private moments in her room, *I will simply burst. I'll come apart like a dropped cup and be useless.*

She parted the curtain to see if maybe she could hike over to Becky's house. All those children would make the hours fly past. But the wind had begun to howl and toss broken limbs about like leaves.

She smelled the bread baking and returned to the kitchen to assure herself it wasn't burning. It wasn't. Out of excuses for staying away, she joined Ben and Mrs. Twining in the parlor.

"We could play charades," Ben suggested.

"No fun with only three people." Lily shuddered. "I am no actress."

"Well," Mrs. Twining said. "We can play word-guessing games. I think up an object, and you ask questions to try to figure it out."

"Pa and I used to play this." Ben settled

back on the sofa. "It passed hours on the road. You can say only yes or no to the questions."

"And maybe we should ask only a certain number of questions." Lily thought the game sounded like a good way to avoid talking about more personal matters with Ben. "Whoever guesses correctly, wins. You start, Mrs. Twining."

"I have it." She wrapped her cane on the floor like a starting gun for a race. "Ben, first question to you."

"Is it in this room?"

"Yes."

"Is it warm?" Lily asked.

"Yes."

"Can it ever be cold?" Ben tossed in his question.

"Yes."

"Fireplace!" Lily and Ben cried together. Mrs. Twining laughed. "No."

They took turns asking questions, neither of them guessing again.

"Is it bigger than the ceiling?" from Ben.

"No."

"Smaller than the lamp?" from Lily.

"No."

"Does it ever leave this room?"

"Yes." Mrs. Twining gave one *bang* with the cane. "Your questions are up. Any guesses?" Ben and Lily shook their heads.

"It's the two of you." Mrs. Twining smiled. "The two people I love best."

"Oh. Well . . . Thank you." Lily blinked, but fearing she might cry, she leaped from her chair and raced to the kitchen.

The bread was finished. She rolled up her cuffs to protect the sleeves of her second-best dress, removed the loaves from the oven, and gave the stew a stir. Fragrant steam wafted into the room. She tasted the concoction, added a pinch more salt and a dash of pepper. Voices drifted to her from the parlor, the words indistinct, their nearness a comfort.

She wouldn't have that in the city. She would be alone, which was why she had believed she could persuade Matt to move to the city, as well. She didn't want to be alone again as she had been on the farm after her family died.

"But you won't be." She gave herself a quiet scolding. "You will have people all around you all the time. It's what you want."

But Mrs. Twining was old and had lost all but one member of her real family. She had taken Lily in. Lily knew the older woman would not stop her, yet leaving her felt a little like betrayal. Mrs. Twining cared enough to understand Lily's restlessness, her need for activities Browning City couldn't provide.

And Ben? He would keep her there because he cared about her.

Unable to face him across the parlor again, catch him gazing at her, smiling at her, reaching his hand out to her, Lily chose to remain in the kitchen. She could make a sweet to go with the stew and bread.

She entered the pantry to inspect the shelves. The previous autumn, she had preserved jars of wild berries. With those, she could make a cobbler or jellyrolls, or she could spread them warm on a plain cake. She would think of something to make from the ingredients at hand. No eggs. That meant a cobbler. Maybe she should use apples if they had any left.

Standing on tiptoe, she reached for the highest shelf where she had stowed last year's apples. Her fingertips brushed against the wrinkled side of a fruit. She could get a chair, but with a little more height, she could reach it now. . . .

She grasped the edge of the preserves shelf for balance.

And it collapsed.

Lily screamed. Wood cracked. Jars shattered, spraying the walls, floor, and Lily with shards of glass and rivers of sticky fruit.

Blackberry juice ran down the front of her second-best dress, staining it, ruining it.

Lily burst into tears.

"Are you all right?" Ben bolted into the kitchen and drew Lily away from the glass. "Lily, are you hurt? Where? Oh, my dear, I can't see where you're cut."

"I'm not." Lily found herself sobbing against his chest, and his arms holding her close. "It's the mess. The fruit. My dress."

"Is that all?" He nudged her chin up and smiled down at her. "I was sure you received a mortal wound. But it's just some fruit and a dress."

"Just? Why you, you — oh."

Ben kissed her, driving distress, annoyance, and everything but love for him out of her head.

NINE

"I–I'm sorry." Ben leaped back a step but kept his gaze on Lily's face.

Her flushed face.

"I mean, I'm not sorry for my sake, but you — uh . . ." He shoved his hands into his pockets. "I shouldn't have done that."

"No." Lily pressed her fingers to her lips and closed her eyes. "We scarcely know each other. We — I . . . Oh." Her hand still against her mouth, she fled from the kitchen.

A moment later, a door closed with a decided bang.

"What was I thinking?" Ben raked his fingers through his hair.

He wasn't thinking. That was the problem. He'd let his natural instincts take over his good sense and given in to temptation. He would consider himself a blessed man if Lily so much as looked at him again, let alone talked to him.

Now that the storm had ceased save for the wind, he figured he should go home. Yet he didn't want to face Great-Aunt Deborah at the moment, and he couldn't fetch his coat without going through the parlor. Besides, he couldn't leave the mess on the floor. Cleaning it up would take some hard labor.

Just what he needed.

He stepped over the glass and preserves to fetch a broom. Behind him, he heard the *thump, thump, thump* of Great-Aunt Deborah's cane.

"What happened — aah."

Slowly Ben turned to face Great-Aunt Deborah. "It's worse than this." He felt his face heat. "I — uh — kissed her."

"Did you?" Great-Aunt Deborah's faded blue eyes brightened with a twinkle. "Imprudent, but understandable."

"She doesn't understand." Ben decided the mess was too sticky for the broom and stooped to gather glass fragments and dump them onto an old newspaper. "It's bound to push her away."

"It may." Great-Aunt Deborah lowered herself onto a kitchen chair. "And you'll have to let her go. But it might bring her back if things don't work out the way she wants them."

"Might." Ben flung a large chunk of glass onto the pile, scattering the smaller slivers. "It only took me five weeks to realize I'm in love with her. Why should it take another man longer?"

"She's lived here for three years without marrying."

"Because no one wanted her for his wife?"

Great-Aunt Deborah sighed. "Probably not. She's made it so clear all along that Browning City is merely a stopping place for a while that most young men keep their relationships with her as friendships."

"Wise of them." Ben gathered up the glass and stalked to the back door. "I should have listened to you about Lily. But I thought . . ." He allowed his words to die as he shoved into the frigid night and deposited the splintered jars in the trash bin.

He was a fool to think he could change Lily's mind. Of course he could not. He had too little to offer her. Yes, he worked in a good position, but he had no real home. Yes, in five years or so, he could save enough money to afford a farm and a few years after that, provided the harvests remained strong, a house worthy of a wife and family. In the event he won the plowing contest, he might shave off a year or two of that waiting time or build a house right away instead of waiting another half a decade after purchasing a farm. Either way, he could never give Lily the life she wanted, never provide her with pretty things and travel nor a host of people around her and occasional adventures.

All he had to offer her was his love.

Unless he found the gold.

He returned to the house to find Great-Aunt Deborah pouring water into a pot to heat.

"Only hot water and strong soap will get that up. I'll let you do the scrubbing. It's not men's work, and Lily made the mess, but it'll be good for you."

"It's the least I can do for her." Ben took the dipper from her. "I'll finish this up, and when I'm done, I'll return to the livery for good."

"As much as I appreciate your being here, I think that's wise." Great-Aunt Deborah returned to her chair. "The less you see of her for a while, the better."

"I'll do what I can to avoid her, but it won't be easy in this town." He thought about how the lack of a variety of people was one of Lily's objections to Browning City and laughed. "I'll wait for her to come to me, if she ever does."

He would also pray a great deal. A great deal more than he already had been praying about Lily, about obtaining money faster, about keeping safe.

He'd added the latter after finding his quarters unlocked. He knew he had locked them, yet wondered if the lock had failed. It was old, the wood around the hasp, worn. Possibly the mechanism sprang under pressure of rain and wind. Possibly.

But not likely.

He'd found an even more secure hiding place for his savings and planned to open an account at each bank the next day. Unfortunately the weather had prevented him from doing so. But it would also keep a thief out. Even so, he worried with the livery empty of his presence except for when he fed the animals. Upon reaching his quarters, he checked on his hiding place first. All appeared well, so he proceeded to feed the horses and mule.

After spending the past two nights with Lily, Great-Aunt Deborah, and himself gathered around the parlor or kitchen fires, he felt the stillness and quiet closing in on him like fog. Outside, the wind howled. Inside, even the animals seemed motionless.

"I used to like this." He spoke aloud to dispel the silence. "I could always feel Your presence better, Lord."

The four walls confined him, made him

restless. He needed open air, a view, the smell of earth warmed from the sun or wet after rain.

Or maybe he simply missed companionship.

"Lord, give me the means by which I can win this woman as my wife."

If he could win her.

The latter thought crept unbidden into his head. He shoved it away. He didn't want to think about the possibility that Lily would never be a part of his life.

Yet that apprehension nagged at his mind in wakeful moments during the night and throughout a Sunday that saw few people attending church.

Lily and Great-Aunt Deborah were two of those who did not arrive at the service.

Concerned, Ben stopped at the house on his way home.

Lily answered the door. "I know. We weren't at church." She offered him a wan smile. "Mrs. Twining didn't think she could walk through this snow and ice, and I didn't want to leave her here alone. You know her. She would try to build up the fire and hurt herself carrying too many logs."

"Thank you for taking such good care of her." Ben glanced around him, seeking something else to say. "And you're all right?"

"Yes, thank you. I just want to get back to work." She gripped the edge of the door. "I'd invite you in, but Mrs. Twining is asleep."

"I understand. I'll pray the wires are up and running for you soon."

So she could earn more money that would take her away from him? What was he thinking?

"Thank you." She started to close the door. "The only good thing about a March storm is the snow doesn't last long."

"I hope not. This isn't good for the livery business, either." He grinned. "Maybe Mr. Gilchrist should buy a sleigh."

He left her smiling in the doorway. His heart rejoiced for that little blessing — he could still make her smile.

Taking Great-Aunt Deborah's advice, Ben steered clear of Lily. With all the businesses closed due to continued ice and snow on the streets in town and the roads leading to Browning City, as well as the railroad, he kept himself busy shoveling, scraping, and hacking ice away from walkways and roofs. In return, the residents kept him supplied with baked goods and dinner invitations.

He saw Lily once in the next three days. Bundled against the cold, she chopped at an icicle hanging from the eave of Great-Aunt Deborah's house.

"Lily." He removed the shovel from her gloved hand. "You're going to send that thing crashing down on your head."

"But it's making the eaves sag." She gestured upward. "Look. I'm afraid we'll get leaks inside."

"You should have asked me to help."

"I didn't know. . . ." She hugged herself. "You haven't been by to see us."

He looked into her eyes. "I thought maybe you didn't want to see me."

"I don't. I didn't. I mean . . ." She shoved her hands up her coat sleeves and stared past his shoulder. "We've missed you."

"We?" He grinned, unable to resist teasing her. "You don't look half big enough for one person, let alone big enough to be two or more."

"Oh, you." She let out a shaky laugh. "You know I meant Mrs. Twining and me."

"Yes, I did, but I wanted to hear you say it . . . Lily." Speaking her name made his insides quiver. Her sudden smile melted him.

"I value you, Ben."

"Thank you."

Not quite what he wanted from her, but a start.

"I heard you were entering the plowing contest and that someone broke into the livery last week." She blurted all the news in a rush. "Why didn't you tell us?"

He shrugged. "I only told one person — Lars Gilchrist. It didn't seem important enough, since nothing was taken."

"But it affected you, so — I mean, we're family." Color tinted her cheeks. "That is, Mrs. Twining is family."

"You were right the first time." He reached out his hand, stopped short of touching her. "Remember? We included you in our little family."

"That was kind of Mrs. Twining and you, but I'm afraid . . ." Her hands knotted inside her sleeves. "I need to get inside. My feet are freezing. May I offer you coffee?"

"No, thank you. I'm having dinner with the Gilchrists tonight and need to go get on some clean clothes."

"That's good of them to invite you." She turned toward the door, showing him only her profile. "Eva is as nice as she is pretty."

"Yes, she is."

Ben wanted to shout with joy at Lily's reaction to the news he was having dinner with Eva and Lars Gilchrist. Every tense line of her body proclaimed how little she liked the image of him across a table from the lovely blond.

She did care for him.

But he couldn't leave her thinking he and Eva might end up courting. Lily might leave town sooner.

"Tom Bailyn will be there, too," he added.

"Oh." Her shoulders relaxed. Her chin line softened. "I'm sure you will enjoy yourself. They have a housekeeper since Mrs. Gilchrist died last year. She's a wonderful cook."

"I doubt she makes bread as good as yours."

She smiled at him. It kept him warm on the walk home.

He would have jogged if ice didn't still create treacherous patches along the route.

Instead, he whistled while feeding and grooming the stock, hummed as he cleaned up and changed into fresh clothes, and sang aloud as he locked both doors of the livery and, lantern in hand, trudged through the night to the largest house in Browning City, that of Lars Gilchrist.

Fog rolled up from the river a mile away and across the land to meet him by the time he reached the Gilchrists'. Cold and damp, it was nonetheless a good sign.

"Temperature's rising," he said as he greeted his hostess.

"And by July, we'll be thinking fondly of this cold." Eva smiled. "Come on in, Ben. Rising temperatures or not, it's still chilly out there."

She led him into a parlor twice the size of Great-Aunt Deborah's and containing heavy mahogany furnishings and cushions in a dark red. To Ben, it looked like the lobby of a city hotel, not a home. For a moment, his mind snapped back to those hours spent with Lily and Great-Aunt Deborah, and he wanted to return there. Knowing that was impossible, he settled in to endure the evening.

Good food and dialogue helped. Mostly they discussed business. Being business rivals didn't seem to matter to Gilchrist and Bailyn. They shared frustrations over getting supplies, the quality of those goods they received, and a lack of variety in the products they could offer their customers.

"If I don't get more fabrics in," Bailyn confided, "every lady in Browning City will be wearing the same new spring dresses to the Easter egg hunt and spring bazaar."

"That's why I quit selling dry goods." Gilchrist forked up potatoes as fluffy as thistledown. "I was tired of the ladies complaining."

"And your daughter," Eva said as she handed Ben a plate of sliced bread still warm from the oven. "I think most of us send for fabrics ourselves."

"But it would be so much cheaper if we could purchase it in quantity," Bailyn said.

"Why don't you start selling more dry goods than grocery stuffs?" Ben suggested. "Then Mr. Gilchrist could carry the grocery stuffs."

The other three stared at him.

He gave them a sheepish grin. "My pa was a peddler. We only sold dry goods, so were able to carry a fair bit of choice for good prices."

"It's something to think about." Eva gazed into space and tapped her spoon on the table. "If you hired a seamstress, the ladies who can afford it wouldn't be going into Davenport or out to Des Moines to have their clothes made."

"And men their shirts," Gilchrist pointed out. "Nothing wrong with a seamstress making a man's shirts. I didn't know you had such business sense, Eva."

"I had you as a teacher, Papa."

Gilchrist blushed with obvious pleasure.

Everyone laughed.

"And we didn't know about Ben's knowledge of the dry goods business," Bailyn added in a moment. "You and I should have dinner at the hotel soon and talk more about it."

"Be glad to."

Ben's heart sang with the joy of finding a place where people wanted him, needed him.

His steps jaunty, he left the Gilchrists' house and strode home through fog so thick that moving through it felt like swimming. His lantern swung from his hand and set the mist sparkling like spangles on a circus costume. Despite the chill, he thought he smelled spring's approach in the air.

Like Lily smelling snow.

He smiled and reached for the doorknob to his quarters.

The door was unlocked.

"Lord, please let everything be all right."

Still clutching the lantern, he rushed through to the livery and inspected the horses and mule. They appeared quiet, even sleepy. The mule brayed in protest at being disturbed then turned to his hay. Assured the stock had not been harmed, Ben trudged to his own quarters, steps dragging, and held the light high.

The bed had been heaved aside, the

floorboard torn up.

His savings were gone.

Ten

Pounding on the kitchen door dragged Lily awake. With haste, she flung on a dress, fumbled the buttons closed up the front, and stumbled to the door in her bare feet.

"Who's there?"

"Lily, I'm sorry —"

"Ben?" She yanked open the door. "What in the world?"

"I'm so sorry to disturb you."

He avoided looking at her, and she realized her hair hung unbound down her back.

"What's wrong?" She stepped aside so he could enter the kitchen. "You look ghastly."

His face was white, his eyes dark hollows.

"Did you leave this for me?" He thrust a towel-wrapped bundle into her arms.

"Yes."

It was a loaf of bread.

"Maybe I was prideful to want you to

compare my bread to the Gilchrists' hou—"

"Was the door unlocked when you arrived?"

She reeled under the impact of his harsh question. "Yes, it was. I couldn't have gotten in if —"

"What time was it?"

"What is this about?" She handed the bundle back to him and then snatched a shawl off a hook by the door and wrapped it around her shoulders.

"Please tell me." He dropped the parcel on the table.

The towel opened to reveal a crusty loaf of bread.

Lily's nostrils flared at the aroma.

"About six o'clock. Ben, what is wrong?"

He leaned on the table, breathing hard and staring at her. "The door was unlocked at six o'clock?"

"Yes." She grasped his arm. "Tell me what's wrong."

"I locked it when I left." He bunched his hands into fists. "The last time, I thought I could have been mistaken, but my quarters — Lily." His voice turned ragged. "They took all of my savings."

"Oh no! Oh, Ben." She slid her hand down to curve over one of his. "I didn't even notice the knob. The door was unlocked, but we don't usually lock our doors here, so I didn't think anything of it. I should have gone for the sheriff instead. I should have noticed something was wrong. I should have thought. But I just slipped in and dropped the bread on the table. I felt I was intruding anyway so I didn't look around."

She was babbling.

His hand relaxed beneath hers, though, so maybe the chatter helped him.

"We need to get to the sheriff." She turned to the hall. "Let me fetch my shoes and fix my hair and tell Mrs. Twining. I'll go over there with you."

He shouldn't be alone.

"Thank you."

She heard one of the chairs scrape across the floor as she turned toward Mrs. Twining's bedroom.

The older lady sat up in bed, her face lined with concern. "What has happened?"

Lily told her. "If you think it's all right, I'll go to the sheriff's with him. He's distressed."

"I can understand why he would be." Mrs. Twining shook her head. "All his savings. Why didn't the lad put them in a bank?"

"He didn't know which one to use, and nothing's been open since the last time he thinks he had an intruder." Lily paused in the doorway. "And this is Browning City. We don't have thieves here."

"Not often." Mrs. Twining sighed and looked all of her eighty or so years — old and sad.

"It's the gold," she said. "That rumor about it being in the livery has gone around again."

"But they took Ben's money." Lily cried out the words on a wave of pain. "He'll have to work most of his life to get that money back. He's such a good man; how could God let this happen to him?"

"God does nothing without a purpose, my dear. Now you run along and put some shoes on before you freeze, and go with Ben to see the sheriff, if you can wake him up this time of night. I'll stay here and pray."

"Thank you."

Lily scampered into her own room on lighter feet, the burden slipping from her heart. Yes, having his savings stolen was terrible, yet maybe God's plans didn't include Ben staying in Browning City and buying a farm. Maybe God wanted Ben and her together elsewhere.

She hastened to pull on stockings and shoes and braid her hair; then she dashed into the kitchen.

Ben sat at the table, his head bowed. She opened her mouth to tell him her new revelation, but he glanced up, smiled, and stopped the words at her lips.

His face was calm, peaceful. "I've been praying for the money to be restored."

"And you believe it will happen?" Lily shook her head. "I never got mine back."

"Did you ask God for it?"

"I think I did, but even He can't refill an empty purse."

"Lily, my dear, *God* and *can't* shouldn't be in the same sentence." Ben rose and took one of her hands between both of his. "He can do anything."

She shook her head, not in doubt but in confusion.

"We can talk about it later." He released her hand. "Where's your coat?"

She retrieved it, and they headed for the sheriff's office. Lily's thoughts spun so fast she couldn't think of anything to say. Ben didn't attempt to make conversation, either. She suspected he continued to pray.

She wanted his prayer to be answered for his sake, for the sake of such wonderful faith, such assurance that all would be well. Life never worked that way for her. In the past few years, God seemed to take from her, not give — her family, her pay, Ben.

She had been foolish to imagine he would move to the city now that he had lost his savings for the farm. He believed God would restore his money, and though Lily feared he was right, she couldn't imagine how.

Heart heavy, she reached the sheriff's office with Ben. The building, like the town, lay dark and still beneath a blanket of fog. Ben pounded on the door then took the lantern around back to the lawman's quarters. A few minutes later, a sleepy-eyed Sheriff Dodd pulled open the door and let them in.

"I don't know what I can do for you, Purcell." He began poking at embers glowing in the stove. "No way to find a thief tonight, not in this fog."

"You do need to be aware that we have a thief in Browning City."

Lily didn't miss how Ben said *we,* as though he already felt a part of the town.

"Never have done before you came." The sheriff rubbed his bristly chin, the rasp grating in the quiet. "Course, no one was ever shot until you came along, either. Not to my recollection anyhow."

"I had money stolen from the telegraph office." Lily jumped to Ben's defense. "So things do get stolen here from time to time."

"That was someone off the train." Dodd sighed. "But I'll make a note of it and ask around. Don't expect anyone saw anything. Clever man to use the fog to cover up his deeds."

"It happened before six o'clock," Lily persisted. "I delivered some bread to him, and the door wasn't locked."

"Been dark since about that time with this weather." Dodd shook his head. "Nobody was about, I'm sure."

"But —"

"Just thought you should know." Ben slipped his hand under Lily's elbow and guided her out of the office.

Once the door closed behind them, she turned toward Ben. "He thinks this is all your fault."

"Yes, he does. He thinks I brought an enemy with me." Ben set off at a brisk pace despite the low visibility, drawing Lily along with him. "But I never stayed anywhere long enough to make enemies."

"Or friends."

"Or friends."

"But you've only been here for a month and a half, and you've already made lots of friends."

He laughed without humor. "Lily, I never stayed anywhere for a month and a half.

Three weeks for the spring plowing in farm country and four weeks in Chicago to settle up Pa's bills after he died."

"At least you were around lots of people."

"People, yes. Friends, no." Ben squeezed her arm. "But not all of them were unkind. I'd been attending a church. One of the men helped me sell our supplies, and a few of the ladies brought me food."

"So it wasn't all bad."

Lily found she needed to know the answer to that with an urgency that scared her. All she had been able to think about after her parents and then brother died and she sat alone on a farm miles from anyone was the notion of people, noise, light. The more the better. Browning City — as far as the stagecoach had brought her with the coin she could spare for travel — seemed like a haven. People had been kind, sympathetic, helpful in a practical way. But still too quiet, especially on nights like this when the weather kept everyone indoors. Since the deaths of her last family members left her alone and isolated on the farm, silence had frightened her, but now she wondered if being alone in a crowd could be just as bad.

"No, it wasn't all bad." Ben's voice sounded thoughtful. "I might have found a place there to settle if I hadn't run across

Great-Aunt Deborah's name in Pa's papers. Leaving the city and coming here seemed the right thing to do after that."

Lily caught the edge of doubt in his tone.

"But now you're not sure?"

"It does seem someone doesn't want me here."

We all want you here.

Fortunately for Lily's sake, they reached Mrs. Twining's house before she gave in to temptation and spoke those words aloud.

Ben took her hand in his at the door. "Thank you for coming with me."

"It didn't do any good. He didn't want to hear about what time I was there or anything."

Ben chuckled. "I think he takes crime in his town as a personal offense against him. He'd rather ignore it."

Lily sighed, said good night, and slipped inside. When she told Mrs. Twining about what happened at the sheriff's office, she nodded in understanding and said about the same thing as Ben.

"If those gold thieves hadn't come through here after the war," the older woman concluded, "we probably wouldn't even pay a sheriff."

"Mrs. Twining, ma'am . . ." Lily hesitated, but since she had already begun, she couldn't back out now. "Do you think — I mean, I know you don't like to talk about it, but do you think this person could have been looking for the gold in the livery and just run across Ben's money and taken it instead?"

Mrs. Twining closed her eyes and nodded. "I'm afraid it could have happened that way." She held out one hand. "Will you pray with me that we are able to set these gold rumors to rest once and for all?"

Lily joined her in prayer but believed the only way to stop the legend and the gold seekers was to find the treasure.

"Mary Reeves is taking up a collection for Ben," Becky said as she greeted Lily at the door.

"A collection for Ben?" Lily shucked off her coat, almost too warm in the balmy spring weather that had descended on Browning City that Wednesday before Palm Sunday. "Why?"

The moment she asked the question, she realized it wasn't kind of her.

"You mean to replace what was stolen?" she concluded.

"Yes, and she has nearly enough to replace what was taken." Becky hugged Lily. "Isn't that wonderful? People here are so kind and generous. It's no wonder Matt decided to stay. And Ben, too."

Becky's announcement slammed into Lily.

"Yes, no wonder." Lily felt as flat, as colorless as she knew she sounded.

The town was replacing Ben's savings. Ben, who had been there for less than two months. Ben, who had a well-paying job and a place to live along with that job. Ben, who got invited everywhere to dinner because he was an eligible bachelor, so he didn't have to pay for much food. Ben, who had family.

Lily swallowed an enormous lump in her throat and forced herself to smile. "I guess he can stay here if he wants to and not have to wait a dozen years to buy a farm."

"I hope so." Becky grasped Lily's arm and drew her into the kitchen. "He's such a nice man. He must have shoveled out half this town after the storm. But you probably know more about him than the rest of us do." She winked.

Lily blushed and turned to the sound of running feet. She braced herself in time to meet the onslaught of two little girls with flying dark pigtails.

"My two favorite ragamuffins." She hugged them close. "I have presents for you."

"Goodie. Goodie."

The girls jumped up and down.

"It's 'Thank you.' " Becky smiled along with the reproof.

"But she hasn't given us anything yet," said Molly, the younger.

"That was rude, Moll," her elder sister by a year scolded.

Lily laughed and pulled tiny scraps of lace from her pocketbook. "Hats for your dolls. For Easter, of course."

"Yea!"

They started to rush from the room, halted as if caught up on strings, and raced back to hug Lily again.

"Thank you, Miss Lily."

Then they dashed off again.

"You spoil them." Becky began making coffee.

"I always wanted little sisters." Lily began to sort through materials they had collected to decorate the church hall for the Easter egg hunt. "I was the youngest and didn't like it."

Becky flashed a grin over her shoulder. "Maybe you should just have children."

"Becky, for shame." Lily felt her neck grow hot under her knot of hair. "I need a husband first."

"Of course you do." Becky started laughing. "I mean, the husband is easy from what I hear."

"Then you hear more than I do," Lily snapped.

"Calm yourself." Becky laid her hand on Lily's shoulder. "Has something upset you? I was only teasing about Ben. We all know he's head over heels for you."

"I don't want to stay here. He does. That's the end of it."

And people wanted him to stay.

"I can take a hint." Becky picked up a sheet of tissue paper and began to fashion a flower. "I'll talk about Matt instead. I never thought he'd look at me, not with you around, but he . . ."

Lily let Becky chatter on and on about Matt. It kept her from having to say anything as they made flowers and paper chains, drank coffee, and chuckled over eruptions of childish laughter from the other room.

At nine o'clock, Becky's oldest brother, a gangly youth of fifteen, sauntered into the kitchen. "Ma says I should walk you home, Miss Lily."

"Thank you, Devlin, but I may need to make a stop along the way."

Lily shrugged into her coat, hugged Becky good-bye, and stepped into the night, a silent Devlin beside her.

A heaven of stars arched overhead. Bright. Clear. Romantic. This was a night to share with a beloved.

Lily wrapped her arms across her body and trudged two streets over to the parsonage. She knew it was getting late to make a call. She also knew that Jackson and Mary never turned anyone from their door, regardless of the time.

Except they already had company. Lily spotted shadows through the curtains that indicated several adults in the parlor. She started to turn away.

The front door flew open on a cacophony of voices and laughter, light and movement.

"I'll remember that."

At the sound of Ben's voice, Lily missed a step then quickened her pace. "We'd better hurry, Dev."

"Lily? Lily Reese, is that you?" Footfalls pounded behind her. "Lily, wait up. I want to tell you the news." He caught up and ran around to face her. "The Lord did provide for returning my money. Isn't that wonderful?" He picked her up and swung her around.

Mirth erupted from Devlin and the house behind him.

Ben released her like the wrong end of a

hot poker. "I apologize. I was so happy I forgot myself."

"I can understand why." Despite her aching heart, Lily laughed at his enthusiasm and antics. "You have amazing faith."

And she burst into tears.

"Lily. Lily, honey, what's wrong?" Ben slipped an arm around her shoulders and guided her to the house. "Come back here and sit down. Mary?"

"Yes, bring her in." Mary held the door wide.

The other guests and Devlin had discreetly gone on their way.

"What is it, sweetheart?" Mary pulled a handkerchief from her pocket and pressed it into Lily's hand. "Did something or someone hurt you?"

"Yes. No." Lily gulped and got herself under control. "I'm sorry. I'm sorry. I should go home now."

"I don't think you should." Ben pressed her hand. "But I'll leave you here with Mary and Jackson unless you want me to stay."

Lily did want him there. Nothing had felt better than his arm around her and him by her side, a bulwark of strength and comfort. Yet what she wanted to discuss with Mary concerned him.

"If Jackson doesn't care," Ben said, "I'll

stay with him in his office so the two of you can talk alone. Then I'll be here to walk you home, Lily."

"Thank you." Lily gave him what she feared was a wan smile.

"Such a thoughtful man." Mary gave Ben a warmer smile. "I'll take Lily into my sewing room."

She led the way to a small chamber boasting more books than sewing supplies. It also contained two armchairs. She indicated one for Lily and took the other herself.

"Now tell me what has you so upset."

Lily bit her lip. Now that she had someone to whom she could express her reaction to Ben's good fortune, she realized how selfish she sounded. But who better to admit that to than the pastor's wife?

"I'm confused." Lily twisted her hands together on her lap. "This isn't nice."

Mary smiled. "I didn't think it would be. People don't usually get upset about nice things."

"No, but I mean — it makes me look . . . mean."

"I can't imagine you being mean, Lily." Mary reached forward and patted her hand. "Just talk."

"I'll try." Lily took a deep breath. "Last year, when I had my wages stolen, no one did anything to repay me. And I'd been here for two years. Ben is here for less than two months, and you organize a scheme to get donations."

"Aah."

Other than that one sound, Mary said nothing for so long, Lily wondered if she should leave, if the pastor's wife had given up on a poor-spirited and selfish woman like Lily Reese.

"Thank you for being honest with me," Mary said at last. "I can see why you might be hurt by that."

"It seems rather unfair." Lily heard the anger in her tone and bowed her head in shame.

"I think you're right. It does. But I'm going to be honest with you, my dear."

Lily looked up. "Why do you all deem him so much more important than you do me?"

Mary met and held Lily's gaze. "First of all, I didn't begin this collection. A few people came to me because Ben helped them out so much during the storm. People here aren't wealthy, but they're not poor, either, and they're generous with what they have. Ben was generous with his time and strength, and many people here, including businessmen, owed him for all the shoveling and scraping he did to clear the walkways and roads. He let people feed him, but he wouldn't take pay, even though we all know he wants to save enough money for a farm and settle here."

"I've done a great deal for this town, too. I organize the spring bazaar, the Christmas pageant, the harvest . . . any number of things."

"You do, and we appreciate all of them." Mary sighed. "But, Lily, you make it clear you do these things because you like entertainment, noise, and lots of people around you."

"And what's wrong — ?" Lily caught her breath. Twin tears rolled down her cheeks. "You're saying that I am doing these things for myself and not others."

"Tell me if I'm wrong."

"I . . . can't."

Lily remembered her reasons for cleaning up Ben's quarters, making the room habitable. She had done it for herself, not for Ben.

She wanted to crawl under a table and hide. Better yet, take the next train out of Browning City before anyone learned how awful she was.

Except they already knew.

She wiped her eyes on her sleeve. "So you all didn't help me out when my wages were stolen because I'm selfish and you don't like me much."

"On the contrary, my dear." Mary's voice broke. "We love you very much, and we knew that the sooner you got enough money saved, the sooner you would leave us. If we had thought that loss was a true hardship, we would have helped and then some. But we don't want you to move east, where you don't know anyone and won't have a spiritual home and friends and family to support you. We want you here where we can love and protect you and give you the spiritual food you need to grow."

"But this isn't my home or my family. I lost those." She cried the words straight from her heart. "I was so alone, and everything was quiet. . . ." She began to sob.

"Oh, my dear." Mary knelt before Lily and clasped her hands in hers. "You weren't alone. God was with you. You simply needed to ask Him for help. Do you ever do that?"

Lily shook her head. "Not for myself. I pray for other people, but He doesn't want to help me."

"Of course He does." Mary snatched a piece of calico from the sewing table and handed it to Lily, who wiped her eyes on the colorful fabric. "He's with you every minute of every day. He wants to guide every step of your life and promises to see to all your needs. But He asks us to trust Him and give our hearts to Him. Have you done that, Lily? Have you given your heart to the Lord?"

"I asked Him to forgive my sins a long time ago."

Mary smiled. "That's a good start. But He wants you to give your heart to Him, too. Give Him your life and all your desires and trust Him. Can you do that?"

"I . . ."

What if God wanted her to stay in Browning City?

Suddenly Lily couldn't breathe. She wanted to bolt from the room, run from the house, and keep on moving until she no longer felt trapped by that one thought.

"I don't know." She couldn't be anything but honest with Mary.

"Will you promise me to think about it?" Mary rose. "And read your Bible."

"Yes, ma'am."

Lily wiped her eyes again and wished she hadn't agreed to Ben's staying around to walk her home. She knew she must look a fright and didn't want him to see her that way.

But when she and Mary walked into the hallway and Ben and Pastor Jackson stepped from the office, Ben gave Lily such a warm smile she thought maybe she didn't look so bad after all.

"You ready to go home?" he asked.

She nodded. "Mrs. Twining will be worrying."

"Not Great-Aunt Deborah. She doesn't worry about anything. She just prays about it."

"She is a tower of spiritual strength in this town," Jackson said. "I have no doubts that her prayers brought you here, Ben. And will keep you here, too, the Lord willing."

"I'm praying He is." Ben shook the pastor's hand, nodded to Mary, and offered Lily his arm. "Shall we go?"

They walked into the night, arm in arm like a courting couple. Lily, however, felt anything but romantic despite the warmer air and chandelier of stars. Her heart felt as though someone had torn it free of its moorings and left it to drift about in her chest like an abandoned vessel in a whirlpool. She didn't know what to think and was far too frightened to pray for God's guidance.

Now that I know everyone here thinks I am a selfish beast, Lord, I really can't stay.

Yet she wished she possessed the kind of self-assurance Ben did, despite his vagabond lifestyle and lack of friends because of it.

Lack of friends before he arrived in Browning City.

"Ben," she burst out just moments before they reached Mrs. Twining's house, "will you tell me how you manage to trust that the Lord has the best for you in His plans?"

Eleven

Four days later, Ben sat on Mrs. Twining's hearth rug in the parlor, his Bible on his knee. "I learned to trust in the Lord when I had nothing else constant in my life. Yes, Pa was always there, but he didn't offer me much comfort when I became old enough to understand I didn't have the same kind of life as other boys."

Lily leaned toward him from her position on the sofa. "But how did you learn about giving your heart to God and trusting Him with your future?"

"We didn't travel on Sundays, and sometimes we were near a church." Ben tapped the battered Bible. "A pastor gave me this, and I just started reading. Eventually I started putting the Word together with what preachers said."

"So now you simply know that God will make everything right in your life?"

"I know it. I don't always feel like it."

Lily had struggled with this notion for the four days since her talk with Mary. Ben and she never seemed to have time to talk together, so Lily had picked up her Bible, dusted it off, and tried to read.

"It's just so big I don't know where to start."

"The Gospels are good. So is Romans." Ben began to flip through the worn pages of his Bible. "And Proverbs holds a great deal of wisdom. I like Proverbs chapter three, when I get concerned." He grinned. "*When,* Lily, not *if.* I worry all the time about what my future holds, that God won't do what I want Him to."

"But He restored your savings to you."

"Yes, but I don't know why. I know why I wanted Him to, but I don't know if it's what He wanted." Ben glanced toward the window, where rain streamed down the panes like a waterfall. "It's still not enough for what I truly want, and I may never have that."

Even with his face in profile, she read his longing. She understood it. Her heart hungered, too — and feared. She feared she would never have that which her heart desired.

She clasped her knees. "So how do you go on? I mean, I pray for things like Mrs.

Twining's health and when you were hurt and for sunshine for the spring bazaar. But now I feel like those things were selfish prayers. Now I don't know what to pray."

"Two verses come to mind straightaway." Ben flattened the pages of his Bible and read. " 'Jesus said unto him, Thou shalt love the Lord thy God with all thy heart, and with all thy soul, and with all thy mind,' the twenty-second chapter of Matthew tells us. And Proverbs, chapter three, says, 'Trust in the Lord with all thine heart; and lean not unto thine own understanding. In all thy ways acknowledge him, and he shall direct thy paths.' "

"Those are tall orders." Lily spoke as she tucked scraps of yarn into her Bible to mark those passages. "I don't think I can do that."

"No one can. We need His strength to trust Him. That's really hard to do — admitting we can't do things ourselves."

"But you do," Lily protested.

"I don't all the time." Ben bowed his head. "I didn't when I discovered the theft of my savings. And I'm not sure now that I am trusting the Lord about other things in my heart, things I want that He may not want for me."

"I feel that way, too." Lily folded her hands on top of her Bible. "But even if we are afraid God wants something for us we don't want, should we pray about it? I mean, can we pray for what we want?"

"Yes, of course. He may just close the door on it." He reached out his hand. "What is it you want so badly, Lily, if you can share it with me?"

"A job in the city."

Pain flashed across his face.

"Why?" His voice was soft. "Why do you want to leave us?"

"I don't belong here." She laced her fingers together and held on tight, avoiding his gaze. "I didn't realize how much I was planning all these fetes and parties for my own sake. I said I was doing it for the town. Now I just can't face anyone. I could barely face anyone at church this morning."

"Was anyone unkind to you at church?"

"No. No one treated me any differently. But I feel different."

She felt like her sins had been exposed for all to see. Yet as she thought about it, she realized that her sins had been exposed only to herself. Everyone else already knew why she acted as she did.

"I just can't be a different person and stay here," she burst out. "No one will believe me."

"They will know." Ben gave her an encouraging smile. "But even if they don't, the Lord will, and He's the One who counts. Would you like to pray with me about it?"

"I can't." Lily rose. "Please, let me read and think about this some more. And it's time to get Mrs. Twining up from her nap."

"All right. Just let me or someone know when you want further guidance." Ben rose and went to the door. "I'm having dinner with the Gilchrists again, so I can't stay. But I'll be praying for you. And I'd like your prayers for me, too. I have a number of things to give over to the Lord that I am hanging on to with all my might."

"I can do that."

Praying for him was easy. She didn't have to struggle over the things he desired if they might be in opposition to what God wanted for him. Praying for herself, however, proved difficult at best. During the next week, she read the third chapter of Proverbs several times, committing it to memory. She read the Gospel of Matthew all the way through and started on Romans. The words touched her, yet each time she dropped to her knees to ask the Lord to take her heart and her will, the words stuck in her throat. She could only pray about the fears running through her head.

"I want to find work in the city so I can

go now. I want to go before I love Ben too much to leave."

Speaking the sentiment aloud, she knew she sounded silly. If she loved Ben, she would want to stay with him regardless of where he settled. Yet she knew she could not be happy remaining in Browning City, with or without Ben.

"I feel like I need to go now, Lord. Please provide me with the job I need to do this." She started to rise; then a thought struck her. "And I'm not sure how deeply this goes into my heart, but my head tells me to say, a job if it is Thy will."

Feeling surprisingly better, she got up from her knees and went to bed. After a fine night's sleep, she woke to the cooing of a mourning dove and other less distinct bird-songs. Spring was on its way with daffodils poking their heads from the soil in yellow profusion and buds forming a green haze along the branches of trees.

It was a good time for a new start.

Her footfalls not as heavy as they had been the past few days, Lily headed to the tele-graph office. Something good was going to happen today. She just knew it.

For the first half of the day, nothing out of the ordinary occurred. She sent and received messages. She worked on her crocheting in between those times. She welcomed Theo into the office while she ate her lunch.

Then the second half of her day began with the Morse-coded words: IMPRESSED WITH YOUR WORK STOP WILL YOU COME WORK FOR US IN CHICAGO STOP NOTIFY BY MAY 1 STOP LETTER TO FOLLOW STOP

Lily said nothing of the job offer to anyone. She feared the knowledge would make people treat her differently at the Easter egg hunt on Saturday, and she didn't want a thing to spoil her joy in the knowledge that God had answered her prayer, that He had given her the desire of her heart.

"Maybe I am figuring this out, Lord, and giving You more of my life than I realize."

Bubbling with excitement, she dressed for the party with care. Although sunny, the mid-April day was too cool for a calico dress. She wore her blue wool frock, now with bands of ribbon to cover the preserve stains. While pulling it over her head, she couldn't help but remember the last time she had worn it. She had donned it to be pretty for Ben, and he had kissed her.

She pressed her fingers to her lips. She still believed he should not have done that.

They weren't even courting. Yet for that moment, she felt secure and warm, feelings that proved as fleeting as the embrace.

"Put it aside." She gave herself a scolding for thinking of the incident with anything beyond embarrassment, as she fashioned a bow of ribbon for her hair. She was pinning a crocheted shawl around her shoulders when someone knocked on the front door.

"That'll be Becky and Matt," she called to Mrs. Twining. "I'll be right there."

She smoothed back the wings of hair over her ears and headed for the front door — where Ben stood on the porch with a handful of daffodils.

"They came up behind the livery this week." He held them out to her. "They were so bright and sunny, they reminded me of you."

"How — how sweet of you." Lily's heart did a foolish flip-flop. "Come in and talk to Mrs. Twining while I put these in water."

She buried her face in the sweet-smelling blossoms, loving them, wishing he hadn't brought them. Even more, she wished he hadn't said such a romantic thing to her.

Don't care about me, Ben. I'm leaving. I tell Western Union on Monday.

She tucked the flowers into a glass of water and returned to the parlor. "I have to wait for Becky and Matt."

"No, they went on to the hall." Ben kissed Mrs. Twining's cheek and crossed the room to open the front door. "I told them I'd come fetch you."

"But if we arrive together . . . Ben, you don't understand. That's the kind of thing courting couples do — attending a party like this together."

Ben grinned at her. "So Great-Aunt Deborah has informed me. And as I told her, Becky made the suggestion that I come fetch you."

"And I thought she was my friend." Lily's grumble held no rancor.

Ben laughed. "She's my friend, too." He held out his arm. "May I escort you, Miss Reese?"

"Since I don't want to go alone, I guess I'd better go along with this scheme of Becky's."

"That's not very gracious of you, Lily." Laughter crackled in Mrs. Twining's voice. "You run along and have a good time with my great-nephew."

Lily feared she would.

By the time the adults oversaw the Easter egg hunt and distribution of prizes for the children, she was having a good time. By the time the adult party began, she forgot she objected to attending the party with Ben as her beau. She forgot any grievances and experienced only the joy of playing games and singing with people she had known from two months to three years. People who invited her to be on their teams . . . People who teased her when she failed to score a point, and cheered her when she did . . .

People she realized were her friends.

"As always," Mary told her at the end of the festivities, "you and Becky did a fine job, and we have raised a respectable sum of money for books. Thank you."

"Everyone made it go on well." Lily lowered her eyes from Mary's penetrating gaze. "It's a good way to end a long, hard winter."

"And how are you doing?" Mary asked.

"Better. I'm praying a lot — or trying to — and reading my Bible."

She didn't tell Mary about the job offer.

"See you in church tomorrow."

In church the next day, Lily experienced the true joy of remembering the Resurrection. She always understood its significance, but for the first time, she sensed an uplifting of her heart, the lightening of a burden. She truly praised God with the rest of the congregation — people who cared about her, who hugged her or shook her hand, who sought her out. People who knew her shortcomings and appreciated her strengths.

Who will know me and still care about me in Chicago?

The question gave her pause as she composed her reply to the telegraph company on Monday morning.

And she held off on sending her acceptance.

On Friday afternoon, Lily noticed Ben amid the usual group of businessmen who came to meet the train. He waved at her through the window then turned to say something to Toby, who was racing to reach the office on schedule.

The youth laughed and yanked open the door. "Hurry, Miss Lily. There's someone here to see you."

"I can't leave until you're sitting on this stool." Lily rose and picked up her shawl.

The weather had warmed enough that a coat was no longer necessary except after dark or when the wind kicked up.

"I'm on it. I'm on it." Toby bounded over to the stool. "What time did the train get into the station?"

"Four twenty-six, and it's leaving now."

The whistle blasted through the depot.

"I'll send that on to Des Moines." Toby

began turning the key. "Good night and enjoy your day off tomorrow."

"That's right. It is the third Saturday." Lily laughed at having forgotten she had a day off and exited the office.

Ben met her outside the door. "I was helping Mr. Gilchrist haul some goods down here and thought I'd wait to walk you home." He took her hand and tucked it into the crook of his arm. "I haven't seen you all week."

"I haven't gone anywhere." *Yet.*

"I know. I've been busy spading gardens for Great-Aunt Deborah's friends."

"But not for her?"

"Do you plant a garden?"

Not when I won't be around to tend it.

"I don't have the time for anything more than a few flowers to brighten the place up."

"Maybe she'll let me grow a few vegetables there." As they left the depot, Ben nodded to Tom Bailyn, Lars Gilchrist, and Jake Doerfel; the latter was talking to a stranger. "You can show me how to preserve them, and I'll reinforce that shelf before we put any more jars on it." He grinned down at her.

Lily melted inside at the memory of what occurred after the shelf broke. She shoved the memory away the best she knew how.

"Ben, I won't be here that long."

"You won't?" He halted in the center of the road and faced her. "How do you know that?"

"Because I've had a job offer in Chicago." His face paled as though someone had shot him again.

"When did that happen?"

"The Monday before Easter."

His obvious distress made her throat close.

"I should have known. The inspectors liked you, didn't they?" She nodded.

"I see." He resumed walking, faster, too fast for her to keep up.

"Stop." She tugged on his arm.

"I'm sorry." He slowed. "I didn't want to hear about you going away. I thought . . . When do you leave?"

"I haven't accepted the position yet."

"No? Well, then." He paused and faced her, gripping both of her hands with his, a smile lighting his face in the evening sunshine. "What's holding you back?"

"I — I want to make sure it is what God wants for me."

There, she'd said it aloud.

"I think it's right. I prayed, and the offer came, but I can't bring myself to answer them. I'm not completely comfortable saying yes and making the move. Mrs. Twining needs someone to stay with her, and that'll take time to arrange. And there is the spring bazaar. I have commitments here. And —"

No, she wouldn't admit to him that she wasn't yet certain she could leave him behind.

"I just don't know how to know what the Lord wants for me," she concluded. "I read my Bible a lot now, but I still can't figure this out."

"Then will you come for a drive with me tomorrow?" He tucked her hand into the crook of his elbow again, and they resumed walking. "I asked Mr. Gilchrist if I could borrow one of the buggies and take you out for a drive if the weather is fine. Business is a little slow right now with the spring planting coming up, so he said yes. I know you're free tomorrow. Will you come? I'll provide the picnic, and I think you'll find it easier to seek God's will when you're not distracted by the noise and bustle of town."

"Ben, I . . ." A chill ran up her spine at the idea of going into the countryside, away from even a small town like Browning City. "I hate the quiet, with no people around."

"I'll be there." He covered her hand where it rested on his arm. "That will be enough for a few hours, won't it?"

She feared he was right.

"Can we come back if I don't like it?"

"Immediately."

"Then I'll go."

She regretted the acceptance the instant she said it. But she had agreed, so she would go. She tossed and turned all night, fearing that a few hours alone in Ben's company would tip the scale in favor of her staying in Browning City. But the quiet of the night around her told her she didn't want to stay. She wanted to leave and leave now. She didn't know why she was being so foolish and hadn't accepted the position in Chicago. Oh yes, because she had enjoyed herself so much at the Easter egg hunt and party. She had stayed because she felt responsible for the party arrangements. She stayed because she wanted to celebrate Easter in a church she knew. She stayed because . . . because . . .

She didn't have the courage to leave, just like she hadn't left the farm until the bank sent the sheriff's men to throw her things from the house. Only the things without value, of course. As she'd trudged to the stagecoach stop ten miles away, she vowed to never again live in the country and too far from neighbors to have help in times of need.

But what of the story Ben had told her

regarding his father?

She remembered the tale as she readied herself to go driving with him. The city was full of people, yet no one had aided the older man.

Soon after Ben's arrival, she brought up the subject with him. "If people who live too far apart are strangers, then can people who are too close together be strangers, too?"

"I wouldn't think so over time." Ben assisted her into the buggy and leaped in after her.

A picnic basket took up a good third of the seat. Lily heaved it over her lap so it rested between them.

Ben grinned at her but said nothing about her action.

"Yes," he said as he got the horse moving, "I think one can make friends in the city, especially if you have a church. It just takes longer. People don't seem to be as trusting."

"That's a comfort to think about." Lily tilted her head back to feel the warmth of sunshine on her face. "When I was growing up, we didn't have many neighbors. They were far away, and we spent most of our time with just the family. Three generations of us."

"Did all of them die in the epidemic?" Ben asked in a quiet voice.

Lily shook her head. "No, Grandmomma just got old. Then Momma . . . I don't know what took her. She just got real tired and pale and slipped away from us about a year before the typhoid took Daddy and my brother. The other women in the area were older and busy with their own families. I didn't have any females my age to talk to until I came here."

"And gentlemen callers?" Ben flashed her a grin.

She ducked her head so the brim of her bonnet hid her face. "There were one or two of those. But I couldn't leave Daddy and Owen, my brother. And it's too nice a day to talk about those kinds of things. Where are you taking me?"

"To the piece of land I am going to buy."

"Oh." Lily shuddered.

"It's only six miles out of town."

"Too far to get in on a weeknight."

"I expect so."

Ben steered the buggy around a farm wagon filled with children. He waved to the man and woman on the seat. They and all of the children waved back.

"Who are they?" Lily asked.

"The people who own the farm next to

the one I want." Ben rested one elbow on the picnic basket. "It's not large, but it runs along the river and has a good stream for water. There was a house there once, but it burned down a long time ago. It's uncultivated land except for grass, of course, and trees along the creek."

"It sounds pretty," Lily murmured.

"You sound dubious."

"Why are you taking me there?" she asked, changing the subject.

Ben laughed. "I understand — don't give me too much information about it and tell me what we're doing today. Well, Lily, we are going to enjoy the quiet, each other, this picnic, and the Lord."

Lily squirmed. "The last being first, of course."

"Only if you choose it to be."

She didn't know what she wanted to come first. She knew her enjoyment of Ben's company was the only reason she didn't tell him to turn the buggy around. Yet his certainty that he would purchase this particular piece of land made her wish she had stayed in town, spending her Saturday off browsing the shops or sitting in the sunshine on Mrs. Twining's front porch and working on lace to sell at the bazaar.

He was so committed to the life of a

farmer that she should steer clear of him forever.

But sunshine, a warm breeze smelling of grass, damp earth, and their picnic fare, and later, when they reached their destination, the food itself left her drowsy and contented.

"It was kind of Mrs. Meddler at the hotel to make up that basket." Lily stood up from the rock she'd perched on and began to gather the papers in which chicken, rolls, and berry preserve tarts had been wrapped.

"I repaired one of the hanging wires on that chandelier in the dining room." Ben rose also and held out his hand. "Let's walk."

Lily slipped her hand into his and allowed him to guide her around the property. At the top of a rise, she caught sight of the road in one direction and the river in the other. The road looked empty as far as she could see in either direction. The river foamed in full spring flood between low bluffs. Its roar, muted by distance, and the song of half a dozen birds in the copse of trees by the stream feeding into the river were the only sounds she heard. Not even the ceaseless Iowa wind competed with the Mississippi for its voice to be heard.

"I need to talk." Lily spoke a little too loudly. "The silence makes me crazy. I was so alone on the farm for months. No one to talk to."

"I've been coming out here to talk to the Lord." Ben's tone was quiet. "My voice doesn't feel lost the way it does in the racket of town."

"I think the Lord can hear us no matter what is afoot around us."

"Of course He can." Ben smiled at her. "But can you hear Him?"

"I read my Bible. That's His words."

"Yes, but do His words come to you when you pray?"

"I . . . never thought about it."

"Will you now?" Ben faced her. "Let's take just a few minutes and pray. You have an important decision to make. You don't want to make a mistake."

Because she most certainly did not, Lily agreed. With Ben, she knelt on the grass, inhaled the sweetness from their crushing the tender stalks, and began to silently talk to God. *Lord, I can't live like this, yet I am not sure I have the courage to leave after all. I don't have an answer from You yet. Please give me an answer that makes sense to me. I can't live this far from people. This land is pretty, but I am so scared of the quiet. I don't like it. I can't —*

She stopped. She heard her voice in her

head, and it wasn't a pleasant sound.

She sprang to her feet. "I want to leave — now."

"Now?" Ben blinked up at her. "It's early still, and I want to walk down to the river."

"Now. If you won't drive the buggy, I'll walk." With that, she turned and strode for the road.

Ben caught up with her. "Lily, what's wrong?"

"What's wrong? I sound whiny. I'm whining to God about what I can't do and don't want." She squeezed back tears. "I can't give up anything to Him — surrender."

"I understand." Ben clasped her shoulder as they reached the buggy. "I'm struggling with that myself."

"What can't you surrender to God?" Lily demanded.

Ben dropped his hand away. "You."

He left her side to fetch the hobbled horse. When he returned, Lily still had thought of no response. She trembled inside as though she had not eaten the hotel's delicious chicken and tarts. Emptiness gnawed at her.

Ben finished harnessing the horse to the buggy. "Need a hand up?"

She shook her head, stepped on the wheel, and swung herself into the buggy. It shook beneath her. She glanced down. The ground was soft, not too wet. Perfect for plowing. It was a fine place to farm.

Some lady would be happy to work the land at Ben's side.

Lily hugged herself and stared straight ahead.

Ben climbed in beside her, and the buggy rocked. "I should have found more stable earth to leave this on. We'd better get going."

They headed for the road. The buggy rattled and creaked beneath them. Ben frowned but said nothing. Lily remained silent, too. She felt ill in the badly sprung buggy on an even worse road.

Except the drive out hadn't felt so bad. Of course, they were traveling a bit faster now, perhaps. She suspected Ben wanted to be free of her as fast as she wanted to be away from him.

That was wrong, though. She didn't want to be apart —

The right wheel dropped into a rut.

"Ouch."

"I'm sorry. This isn't handling —"

A *crack* splintered the quiet.

"Hang on!" Ben shouted.

But she had nothing to hang on to as the right wheel broke loose. It spun away in one direction. Lily flew in another. Pain roared through her skull until blackness took over.

TWELVE

Lily came to consciousness with a groan. If she hadn't heard herself, she would have believed she had lost her hearing. Silence lay over everything else like fog. She tried to open her eyes, but the lids remained too heavy, weighed down, she suspected, by smaller versions of the rock that had become her pillow.

Why did she have a rock for a pillow?

She tried to raise her left arm. Pain screamed along her shoulder. She lifted her right hand. Little discomfort. Much better. She touched her face. No stones on her eyelids. Just fatigue. She needed more sleep.

Another groan jerked her from her torpor. That wasn't her voice. Forcing her eyes open, she found she wasn't at Mrs. Twining's. She lay on the road. Remains of the wrecked buggy lay strewn a few yards away, with no sign of the horse in the shafts. Beyond that, she saw Ben crumpled like a heap of discarded laundry.

"Ben." She tried to stand.

Her legs collapsed beneath her. Barely, she caught herself from landing on her face.

"Please, Lord."

She didn't even know what to pray. One thought filled her head — get to Ben.

She crawled. Stones grinding into her hands and knees, she scuttled across the road to where Ben lay.

Where he lay too motionless and quiet to have groaned.

Her heart racing, Lily touched his neck. She found no pulse. His skin felt clammy.

Memory of a fetid room, cold skin, and silence swept through her. She was alone again. Ben had left her utterly alone with no one to help her. Everything, everyone she cared about had vanished once more.

She opened her mouth to scream.

You weren't alone. Mary's words stopped Lily's cry. *God was with you.*

"Are You there, God?" she called. "Ben really needs You right now."

Unless nothing could help him now.

Tensing, she moved her fingers on his neck and felt his pulse. It was weak, irregular, but it was there. She glanced around him, touched his scalp. She saw no blood, but she found a lump on the back of his head.

"Ben, can you hear me?" She ran her fingertips across his forehead. "Open your eyes for me."

He didn't move.

"Ben, you brought me out here. Don't leave me alone." She started to cry. "I don't know what to do out here. I can't call for help."

God was with you.

God is with you.

"How can I know that?" She covered her face with her hands. "I pray for answers, and You let this happen. You leave me alone out here with someone who's too quiet. You've left me." Her voice grew hoarse, her sobs ragged. She was whimpering, accusing God of . . .

Doing something He had promised never to do — leave her.

Lily caught her breath and stared at a cloud drifting across the sky. Her head spun, so she rested it on her updrawn knees. She was reaching for something, a fullness, an understanding, an answer she knew she could reach if only her head didn't feel like an overripe melon.

God promised never to leave His people. Yet she felt abandoned. How could that be, since the Lord's Word was truth? Logic . . .

Logic . . .

If God never left, and yet she never felt His presence even in her prayers, then she must have . . . must have . . .

Become absent from God.

"I've abandoned You." She hugged her knees tight to her chest. "I prayed, but I never really believed. I never truly gave up my heart to You."

As she had done with fixing up Ben's quarters and arranging parties to raise money for good causes, she had gone through the appropriate motions with God while her heart had been selfish. She filled up her life with work and play instead of devotion to the Lord.

"I need a whole lot of forgiveness, Lord," she whispered into the quiet. "I —"

"Lily?" Ben's voice interrupted her.

"Shh. I'm listening to my heart."

Ben chuckled then fell silent.

The world lay in stillness. Even the wind seemed to hold its breath while Lily stumbled through a prayer of surrender to the Lord. The quiet seeped into her mind, her heart, her soul. The shakiness vanished.

She raised her head and gazed into Ben's eyes.

"Good afternoon."

His voice sounded rough. His eyes weren't

quite focused. Dirt smeared his face.

"Are you in pain?" she asked.

"Not when I look at both of your beautiful faces."

She giggled. "That isn't a good sign."

"Can you walk to town for help?"

"I can, but I won't leave you." She brushed his hair back from his brow. "It's Saturday. Someone will come by soon."

"You're not afraid of us being alone until they do?"

"We're not alone." She smiled down at him. "The Lord is with us."

Two days later, Ben straightened from his examination of the buggy wreckage. Some of the dizziness that had plagued him since the accident swept over him, and he swiped his sleeve across his brow.

"It was no accident." Ben frowned at Lars Gilchrist. "Someone tampered with the axle."

"How can you be certain?" Mr. Gilchrist looked old and tired. "Could it not have broken from age and poor repair?"

A twinge of anger plucked at Ben's gut.

"I keep everything in good repair, sir." He poked the pieces of axle with the toe of his boot. "It's been cut."

"It's not simply a flaw in the wood?"

"And a piece is missing."

Gilchrist scowled. "Why would someone take a piece of the axle?"

"It's a shorter piece from the wheel to the main shaft. This is long, but it's not long enough."

"It could have fallen somewhere else." Mr. Gilchrist glanced about the empty countryside where the accident had occurred. "The wheel rolled a good ways away."

"Yes, sir, and the piece had been cut from it by the time we all got back here. Two days is more than enough time."

"But why would someone want to do that to you and Miss Lily?" Gilchrist began to pace back and forth across the narrow road. "It makes no sense to me. You are two of the best young people I know. I can't imagine either of you having enemies."

"No, sir, whatever the sheriff might think." Ben tasted a hint of bitterness in his words and clamped his lips shut before he said more.

"Now, son, he's just trying to keep his town safe." Gilchrist laid a hand on Ben's shoulder. "And you know we had little crime to speak of before you came. It's a logical conclusion for him to draw."

"But I haven't done anything but move here and try to make a new life for myself."

Ben shoved his hands into his pockets and headed for one of the two horses he and Gilchrist had ridden from town. "Before I came here to settle, I'd never stayed anywhere long enough to make enemies."

"So the problem lies somewhere else." Gilchrist joined him at the horses. "We just need to figure out where."

On the way back to Browning City, Ben wondered how to accomplish the task of learning who didn't want him in town and, just as important, why. The idea of Lily being the target was not something to consider. No one could think ill of her.

Of course, Ben didn't know why anyone would think ill of him, either. He didn't believe he was being self-centered to think such a thing. The town had welcomed him. He'd never had an enemy, and no one had ever asked him — or his father — to leave a place. When his father felt the need to move on, they had always gone of their own free will.

His father's free will. Ben had wanted to stay many times, but his father never did, and Ben couldn't let him go alone.

Yet someone didn't like Ben. Didn't like him and wanted to see him gone, maybe even permanently.

Heart heavy, Ben bade good day to Gilchrist in front of the general store; then he returned to the livery, leading the older man's horse. The stable appeared too empty with the buggy missing. The other one stood in its corner across from the plow and other farm equipment. After putting the horses into their stalls, Ben gave the second buggy a thorough inspection. Wheels, axle, single-tree all looked undamaged.

"So how did whoever damaged the other one know I would take it instead of this one?" Ben rocked back on his heels and stared at the vehicle. "How did someone even know I would take out a buggy on Saturday instead of someone else?"

A quick recall told him any number of people could have known the latter. At least a dozen people had seen them drive out of town. Anyone could have followed them and cut the axle while Ben and Lily ate their picnic on the other side of the hill and out of sight of the road. In fact, the perpetrator would have had to carry out his deed in such a manner. Otherwise, the wheel would have broken off sooner, would have come off when they had barely left town.

"What is wrong here, Lord?" Ben spoke aloud in the empty stable.

Empty of people, that is. All but one horse still stood in their stalls. The one missing would be gone the entire week, rented out by a man who didn't like trains and needed to go to Des Moines. Business was slow. Far too slow. With feed and other supplies to purchase, Gilchrist hadn't made enough on the livery to pay Ben's wages.

A hint of fear crept up his spine. Slow business. Someone wanting to harm him or, at the least, scare him off.

"Am I wrong, Lord? Am I not to stay here after all?"

Wind blew the mourning wail of the afternoon train's whistle into town. Ben stood and glanced in the direction of the depot. He should go meet Lily. He hadn't seen her since Saturday. Doc Smythe had ordered both of them to stay in their homes and rest on Sunday, especially Ben, who had seen double for several hours after the buggy wreck. When Ben had stopped at Great-Aunt Deborah's house earlier in the day to ask after Lily, he learned she had gone to work.

"She looked well." Great-Aunt Deborah had smiled. "In truth, Ben, I've never seen her looking better. She looked peaceful."

Ben knew what Great-Aunt Deborah meant. Nothing was quite as beautiful as seeing Lily's face alight with peace and joy. Nothing sounded quite so sweet as hearing her say they were not alone because the Lord was with them.

As he strode toward the depot, Ben praised God for such good coming out of the accident. He hoped her newfound relationship with the Lord meant she would stay in Browning City.

If he was to stay there.

No. He pushed the nagging doubt aside. The attacks on him and the poor business at the livery were not signs from God that he should move on. Surely not. Business would pick up again once the weather stayed fine and planting ended.

As for the attacks on him . . . They must learn who was behind those, especially now that they had risked Lily's safety.

Thinking of Lily lightened his heart again, and he increased his stride. The depot came into sight. A few people headed toward him: some strangers, Tom Bailyn, Jake Doerfel. No sign of Lily.

Ben greeted Tom and Jake then crossed the station to the telegraph office. Lily sat at her machine keying in a message. When she finished, she glanced up at him, smiled, and waved.

"Waiting for Toby," she mouthed.

Ben nodded and leaned against the wall of the office to wait for her. What felt like much too much later, he heard footfalls running up the road and glanced around to see Toby galloping into the station.

"So sorry! So sorry!" he shouted in apology before he reached the office.

Lily shook her head but didn't look in the least upset as she slid off her stool and gathered up her things.

"To what do I owe the privilege of your escort?" she said as she greeted Ben and then spoke over her shoulder, "Toby, I forgot to tell you, the eastbound is running sixteen minutes late at the last report." She took Ben's arm without hesitation and looked up at him. "You didn't need to wait."

"Of course I did." He started walking toward town, thrilled to have Lily at his side.

Where he always wanted her.

"You're awfully patient with his being late all the time. If it's not rude of me to ask, do they pay you extra for waiting?"

"They do, but they've threatened to dismiss him several times." Lily sighed. "But I keep talking the supervisor from Davenport into keeping him on. Maybe I shouldn't let him get away with it, but he is the only wage earner for his mother and five younger brothers and sisters. Their father died in an accident last year. That's why he works a double shift."

Ben covered her hand with his. "I don't know how you could call yourself selfish, Lily." And for his own selfish reasons, he added, "Another operator wouldn't be so generous, staying on, more than likely."

"You mean if I leave."

"Yes."

"You truly want me to stay." She peered up at him from beneath the brim of her bonnet.

"Permanently." He took a deep breath. "I'd like to court you."

"Haven't you been already?" Her tone was light. "The picnic. Taking me to the Easter egg hunt. It looks like courting to everyone."

"Yes, and I want it to be official."

He wasn't being terribly clear, yet he suspected she understood what he meant — he wanted the kind of courting that led to engagement. He wanted, when they knew one another a bit longer — not too much longer — to marry her. He couldn't offer her everything he wanted to, but if she were willing to make do with the quarters behind the livery for a year or two — and if he won the plowing contest this year or next — they could have a fair life together.

No, a good life together.

His mouth dry, he took the next step. "I love you, Lily."

"Oh, my." She tightened her hand on his arm. "Ben, I —"

"I understand if you don't feel the same way. I just had to say it and ask for a chance. But if you don't want to see me anymore now —"

"Shh." She drew her hand from under his and touched a gloved finger to his lips. "I want to spend time with you more than anyone. But at the same time, I — well, I'm afraid. I mean, I could so easily love you. But if I end up leaving, it would only hurt us both."

"Then don't leave." He took her hand in his, and they continued into town with fingers linked. "I thought you wouldn't want to go now. Saturday, you said you weren't afraid of being alone anymore."

"I wasn't. I'm not. But now I know I won't be alone in the city, either. It doesn't mean I have changed my mind about having to be alone, if you understand what I'm saying."

"I'm afraid I do." He sighed to relieve the pain around his heart. "But if you were to stay, I'd have a chance?"

"Better than a chance."

"Then why are you even thinking of leaving?" Stopping, he swung to face her and grasped her other hand. "Lily, if you care about me that much, why would you leave?"

She met his gaze. "You could come with me."

"I have no future in the city." Ben winced at the sadness in her eyes. "My future is here."

"And my future may be in the city." She turned away and resumed walking, Ben falling into step beside her. "I am still waiting to know what the Lord wants for me."

"Isn't time getting short to notify them?"

"Yes. But I have peace that I will know what to do when I need to."

Ben thought about the accident that could have seriously injured Lily, or worse, and had to give in. "I'll wait and pray for you."

"Thank you." She smiled. "And I'll pray that maybe you have a future in the city after all."

"It's not what I want." He glanced around at the houses and businesses beginning to line up on either side of them. "I was born here. My only family is here. But today — Lily, you need to know this. We didn't have an accident on Saturday."

"I beg your pardon? I have a headache that says we did."

"Me, too." Ben grimaced. "What I mean is that someone tampered with the buggy to make it crash."

Lily gasped. Her face paled. "How — I mean, why? I mean . . . Who would want to harm us?"

"Not us, my dear, me."

"But why — oh." A muscle ticked in Lily's jaw. "They're trying to scare you away from the livery."

"I can't help but think that." He knotted his free hand into a fist at anything that so much as appeared to upset Lily. "It's difficult to hunt for gold if I'm living there."

"But rumors of the gold have been around for years," Lily pointed out. "And no one has lived there for even longer than that."

"Someone who is new in town, who just learned of those rumors? Or someone from out of town?"

They turned the corner to Great-Aunt Deborah's street.

"I admit I looked around the livery myself." Ben gave an embarrassed laugh. "Who wouldn't want the reward money for finding that kind of treasure? It would help me buy my farm now instead of waiting several years. And I could make a wife more comfortable than I can now on what I earn. But that place is solidly built. I don't see how anyone could have hidden anything there."

"You had time to look." Lily paused at the end of Great-Aunt Deborah's walk. "No one else can do that." She held out her hands. "Be careful, Ben. I wish . . . Will you think about maybe this being the Lord's way of telling you that you shouldn't stay here?"

When she gazed up at him with her wide, blue eyes, Ben could deny her nothing.

"I'll pray about that, but I can't believe He would bring me here then send me away."

Except maybe to find her?

Now that was something to think about.

"May I see you tomorrow?"

"I think it would be better if we didn't see each other for a few days. Come to Sunday dinner."

"Sunday?" Ben protested so loudly the front curtain twitched back.

He waved to Great-Aunt Deborah then sighed. "You're probably right. Until Sunday." He touched her cheek and strode away at a near jog before he was tempted to do more.

He didn't understand what the Lord was doing to him. He'd prayed for family for years. He prayed for a stationary home and a godly wife. Now he had the former and a wonderful possibility for the latter, and she still talked about leaving.

She didn't love him enough to stay. That

was all there was to it. If she loved him enough, she would give up notions of crowds and bright lights.

If you love her enough, maybe you would give up on open fields and a handful of people.

The thought jabbed him like a knife to his gut. Before falling in love with Lily, he had been so sure settling in Browning City was the right decision, the decision God wanted him to make. Now, he didn't know.

For the rest of the evening, he kept returning to the idea that he was supposed to leave town with Lily. He fought the notion and tried to think of ways he could make staying attractive to her. He knew he couldn't afford to support a wife in style as income matters stood. They wouldn't want for anything, but they would have little for extras, either. Extras like traveling. Lily would be unhappy. Yet in the city, she was the only one of them who would arrive with a job. He could find work, of course, but she couldn't work once they started a family.

"It seems impossible, Lord."

Those were his last words before he fell asleep. The aching place in his head resulting from the accident had spread across his brow and down his neck. He tossed and turned and woke in the middle of the night

with his eyes and nose burning.
From smoke.

THIRTEEN

Lily woke to a clanging bell and the sound of horses pounding along the street, shouts and the smell of smoke. Too much smoke for stove and hearth fires. More like . . .

She shot from bed and stumbled to the window. From her view of the side yard and Mrs. Willoughby's house, she could see nothing. She flung up the sash and leaned out, shivering in the chilly night air, then coughing as smoke billowed into her face on a gust of wind.

The fire was close, but she still couldn't tell where it was. She needed to find the location, carry buckets, help. Everyone in town who could help in a fire did so. They had no fire wagon.

She slammed the window and yanked a dress over her head. Not bothering with stockings, she shoved her feet into her shoes and laced them up. A shawl? No, too easy to catch sparks. Good for beating them out, though.

She tossed one around her shoulders and dashed into Mrs. Twining's room. The older lady sat up in bed, lighting a candle.

"Fire somewhere." Lily's words came out breathless. "I'm going out."

"Of course." Mrs. Twining coughed. "You be careful."

"I will."

"Do you know where the fire is?" Mrs. Twining's eyes filled with concern. "If we can smell this much smoke, it must be close."

"I know."

Lily worried their house might be in danger.

"But it's windy enough to blow the smoke to us."

And carry fire from building to building when they hadn't had rain in days.

"I'll come back if — if we need to leave here." Losing her things was not something to contemplate. All the lace she had made for the bazaar, clothes that were so expensive to replace, her hooks and needles, which cost even more . . .

But others might be losing their things right now. She must hurry, help save what she could.

Lily ran through the kitchen and grabbed two buckets from the pantry. Wind made the back door resist her push to open it. Wind reeking of smoke. Smoke stinging her nostrils and lungs. Too strong not to be a nearby fire.

She threw her shoulder against the door. Another gust of wind sent it crashing back into the door frame. Lily rushed into the night with a black sky overhead and an orange glow to the north.

As she headed toward that glow, she raced past the familiar homes and businesses that occupied that part of town. Dr. Smythe. Not far enough away. Gilchrist's. Still too near. Scott's Bank.

The livery.

Lily broke into a run, tripping and stumbling over uneven ground. "Not the livery. Lord, please, not the livery. Not Ben." More plea than prayer, words poured from Lily between gasps for air.

The livery was only a block away now. It felt like six blocks, like six miles.

She crashed into the first line of a bucket brigade, trying to push past them.

"Lily, stop." Matt Campbell caught hold of her arm. "It's not safe."

"But Ben." She thrust her buckets into

Matt's hands. "Take these. I have to help Ben."

"He doesn't need your help right now." Matt took her buckets.

Someone else thrust a full pail into her hands. "Pass it along, Lily." She did.

"Mary." Lily turned to the pastor's wife. "Where is Ben?"

"With the horses." Mary patted her shoulder then grasped another bucket.

"You're sure?" Lily scanned the scene around her.

Their line passed water from the well of the blacksmith's shop next to the livery. She couldn't see much around the bulk of the smithy shed. Not much more than flames licking up. Shouts, orders from the tone, proved indistinct above clanging pails, roaring flames, and the screams of frightened horses.

She hoped they were only frightened, not injured.

"I can't see anything." Her voice held a hysterical note, and she took a deep breath to calm herself. "Do you know what is happening?"

"Started in the roof, I heard," Matt said. "We're all too busy trying to keep it from spreading in this wind to pay much attention."

"But Ben is uninjured." Mary slid one more bucket into Lily's hand.

Lily took the bucket and the assurance with all the strength she could muster. She must. The town needed every able-bodied person to wet down other buildings and douse the main fire so nothing else caught. She recalled reading about what had happened in Chicago five years earlier. The city burned down — a city with fire equipment, a lake, and a river. The Mississippi was too far away to be of much help. Browning City's founders hadn't wanted to be right on the water in case of flood and to protect against river pirates. They should have thought of fire. Buckets seemed inadequate to subdue the flames. Each load of water seemed to enact no more good than a raindrop trying to put out a stove fire.

"Rain. Lord, we need rain."

She didn't realize she prayed aloud until Mary said, "Amen," in agreement.

"We have clouds," Matt put in. "But not —"

Cries of protest rang from the livery yard, louder than other shouts, a few words distinguishable.

"Stop."

"You can't."

"Leave it."

News rippled down the bucket line. When Lily heard, she wanted to break ranks and go after him, drag him away from the flames, away from danger.

"It's the money." Tears ran down her face like the water dripping down her skirt. "He needs the plow for the contest."

"He needs it badly enough to risk his life?" Mary sounded appalled. "I thought he had more sense than that."

"He does. I mean, he would . . ." Lily was sobbing. "He thinks if he has more money, I'll stay here and marry him. It's not the money. Doesn't he —"

Shouts of relief rang from the livery yard.

"He's safe out," someone at the head of the smithy shed called. "But risking his neck for a —"

A crash and roar of flames and human voices reverberated through the night. A column of sparks soared above the rooftops like upward-shooting stars.

"It's gone," many voices chorused. "Livery's gone."

Ben had just lost his livelihood, his living quarters, and probably everything he owned. Lily wanted to curl into a ball and cry. Yet she was too busy passing buckets of water to succumb to grief or to even think. Her group needed to extinguish the pinpoints of fire landing on the smithy.

Those pinpoints grew to tongues of flame.

"Faster on the water!" a man on a ladder shouted. "I need more water."

"We need rain," Mary said.

And it came; so light at first Lily didn't notice the extra dampness. Then the drops grew fatter and more frequent until she felt as though someone were pouring pails of water over her. Soon the smell of smoke turned into the stench of charred, wet wood. The last of the fires died in a gasp of steam.

"Coffee and food back at the church hall," Pastor Jackson Reeves announced from nearby.

Lily left the bucket line, knowing she could collect Mrs. Twining's pails in the morning, and began to hunt for Ben. With the fire out and rain falling, seeing faces grew impossible. She tried to call to him, but her throat was raw.

She would find him at the hall. He had nowhere else to go unless she found him and told him what she planned.

Along with dozens of other townsfolk, Lily trudged to the church hall. There, with the stove warming the place and making everyone's clothes steam, several of the older ladies had prepared coffee and sandwiches.

Not realizing she was cold until she began to grow warm, Lily accepted a cup of coffee and located Mrs. Willoughby.

"I'll need to stay with you again," she told the older lady. "I'll pay you, of course."

"You're such a sweet girl." Mrs. Willoughby beamed at her. "You know the best thing for that young man right now is to live with his aunt."

"Yes. I think family is where a body ought to be when everything else goes up in smoke." Lily sipped the bracing coffee. "Have you seen him?"

Mrs. Willoughby glanced past Lily's shoulder. "He just walked in."

"Thank you." Lily turned.

If Ben were not so tall, she never would have seen him for the crowd. As it was, she saw only his face, pale beneath a smudged layer of soot. A bruise marred his right cheekbone. His eyelids drooped, and his jaw looked taut. Too taut for a man given more to smiles than frowns. At that moment, he looked like someone who would never smile again.

Lily wove her way through the crowd of sooty townsfolk until she reached Ben. "Here." She gave him her coffee.

"Thank you." He took the cup from her. His fingers brushed hers. His hand was cold, and he didn't smile at her.

"Don't you want this?" He held up the cup.

"I don't need it. I'm going back to Mrs. Twining's house right now to move my things out."

"Out?" Alarm flashed across his face. "But you can't leave yet."

Lily's heart twisted. "Not out of Browning City. I'm moving out of Mrs. Twining's house and into Mrs. Willoughby's so you can stay with family, where you belong."

"Oh, Lily . . ."

His throat worked. He reached out a reddened and blistered hand and laid his palm against her cheek.

"Thank you."

"You're welcome." Lily looked into his eyes, read tenderness replacing the distress, and knew she could never leave his side.

She didn't get any sleep that night. After clearing her things out of her room in Mrs. Twining's house and lugging what she could to Mrs. Willoughby's, she made the effort to bathe and wash her hair to rid herself of the reek of smoke. By the time she finished with drying her hair before the kitchen stove and making breakfast, she needed to go to work. She wanted to get to work. She had the most important telegram of her career to send.

THANK YOU FOR OFFER STOP DE-
CIDED TO STAY IN BROWNING CITY
STOP

The path seemed clear to Ben. With everything he owned except for the plow destroyed in the fire, without a livery to manage, with his heart certain Lily loved him,
he would leave Browning City and hunt for
work in Chicago.

"But I don't want you to just stay here
and manage a new livery," Gilchrist protested at Ben's announcement. "I'd like you
to manage my store, too. I think Tom and
Eva are about to make a match of it, and I
don't want to appear too much in competi-
tion with my son-in-law." He guffawed.

Ben nodded. "That would be awkward,
but now that the two of you are starting to
sell different things, it isn't so bad."

"No, but to tell you the truth, Ben, I
would like to tend to my farm, make it pay
before I'm too old."

The offer tempted Ben. For a moment,
his heart felt torn in two different directions
— stay with a town he had grown to love
and what remained of his family or go to
Chicago to be near Lily until he could ask

her to marry him. He thought of how much he had prayed about his future and all the incidents leading to this moment and shook his head.

"I can't stay, but I am so honored you trust me after all that's happened."

"You didn't start that fire." Gilchrist leaned his hands on the store counter. "Have you talked with the sheriff today?"

"I'm on my way."

Ben wasn't looking forward to that interview.

"I thought I'd talk to you first, in case you wished to come with me."

"No need. You're an honest young man. You'll tell the truth to him just as you did to me."

"Thank you, sir." Ben turned toward the door. "I should get down there."

"If he gives you trouble, you send for — ah, here he comes now."

Sheriff Dodd stepped onto the boardwalk and yanked open the door. He brought the stench of charring with him, and ashes coated his shoes and lower pant legs.

"Saw you through the window, Purcell." Dodd drew his thin brows together. "Thought you were coming to the office first thing this morning."

"I had to find decent clothes first, sir."

Ben discovered he had propped his fists on his hips, and he lowered his arms. "I was just on my way."

"Humph."

"Looks like you've been at the fire site," Gilchrist said.

"Sure have." Dodd glared at Ben. "You don't smoke?"

"No, sir."

"Leave a lantern on?" Dodd persisted.

"No, sir. And the stove was shut."

"Then how did it start?" Dodd's demand emerged like a challenge.

Ben took a deep, calming breath. "Sir, the fire started in the hayloft. I was asleep in my quarters in the back."

"Everyone saw the roof ablaze first." Gilchrist sounded as belligerent as the sheriff did. "If Ben had started it out of carelessness, it would have started below."

"True. True." Dodd sighed and mopped his brow. "I just don't like all these things happening in my town. It was peaceful until he" — he jabbed a finger toward Ben — "came along."

"Or other newcomers," Ben said.

Dodd and Gilchrist stared at him.

"Explain what you mean by that," Dodd commanded.

Ben explained what he and Lily had

worked out about someone wanting to get him out of the livery so they could search it thoroughly for the gold.

"That's ridiculous." Dodd pinched his nostrils as though he smelled something foul.

"Not as ridiculous as you might think." Gilchrist rounded the counter and stood beside Ben. "Nearly ten years ago, a young lady tried shoveling up an entire field in search of that gold. Others have done crazy things to get at it."

"And a body would need to dismantle the place to find anything hidden there," Ben added. "If it is there."

"Hmm." Dodd hooked his thumbs into his belt and gazed at the ceiling as though contemplating the best of the garlic and onions hung there. "Are you suggesting somebody burned down that place to find gold?"

"A man desperate enough for treasure would stop at nothing to get it." Ben spoke softly so as not to break the sheriff's thoughtful mood.

"Hmm." Dodd scratched his chin. "Who else is new in town and started hearing stories of gold in the livery? Not too many folks move here in the middle of winter."

"I don't know," Ben admitted. "Lily Reese

says that it's hard to say sometimes because we do get visitors."

We, Ben had said. As though he would remain a part of this town.

"Only three I know of since October." Gilchrist's lips thinned. "Tom Bailyn, a spinster lady come to live with her sister on a farm about ten miles away, and Jake Doerfel."

"I don't know of any more, really, when I think on it." Dodd laid a hand on his belt where most lawmen carried guns.

He sported a knife in a case and a short, thick club.

Dodd half faced the door. "Let me think on it, and I'll come back."

He strode from the store.

Ben turned to Gilchrist. "He didn't accuse me of burning down the livery to get to the gold that might be there."

"He wouldn't dare. I got him hired. I can get him unhired."

"Thank you."

Ben didn't know what else to say.

"We want you to stay here, lad. And Mrs. Twining sure could use family around in her last years."

"I know, but . . ." Ben hesitated then decided this kind man deserved the truth. "Lily has been offered a job in Chicago. I want to find work there and be close by her until I can support a wife."

"You have a job here and can support a wife just fine." Gilchrist's voice was a growl. "And if she doesn't love you enough to stay here, she isn't good enough for you."

"But she thinks God wants her to go."

"And you? Is it what the Lord wants for you?" Gilchrist gave him a penetrating look. "Or are you thinking of a heart for a woman instead of a heart for the Lord?"

Ben winced. "I wish I knew, sir. I was so sure I'd found the right place here, but everything points to me going. Lily and I wouldn't even have a place to live now if we married."

"You mean because some fool for gold tried scaring you off or killing you off? That doesn't sound like God's message to me, but then I'm not as versed in the Bible as Eva says I should be."

A tingle raced up Ben's spine — excitement, fear, anticipation.

"God uses anyone," he said. "Thank you for your wisdom. I'll think and pray about it."

He left the store to wander through the muddy streets of town. Although rain fell in intermittent bursts, he let himself get wet. He needed fresh air and space to think.

Praying, he discovered, didn't work at the moment. No words would come to him any different from those he had spoken to God a thousand times or more. Yes, more.

He wanted a place where he belonged, a place for roots. Part of those roots should be a wife, children, and family. Yet God didn't seem to want him to have both.

No matter how hard he worked in the city, he could never earn enough to have the kind of home and land he could have here in Browning City, especially if he took Gilchrist's offer after all. If he won the plowing contest, too, he could buy the land before someone else snatched it up.

But he couldn't have these things and Lily, too. Indeed, nothing guaranteed he could have Lily at all.

"Everyone and everything I love gets taken from me." Words burst from him at the edge of town. "Just like Lily."

The earlier tearing of his heart seemed complete. A hollow space lay inside. He had tried to fill it with working hard with Pa, then making a home in Browning City, then the prospect of finding gold, and then the possibility of winning prize money, purchasing land, and winning Lily's heart.

Lily tried to banish her emptiness with noise and activity. He'd told her to fill it with the Lord, yet he hadn't truly done that himself. He yearned for solid things as much as she longed for crowds. He claimed he sought the Lord's direction, but he went in his own.

"Lord, I need Your forgiveness for my willfulness. Thy will be done, not mine."

He didn't know what else to pray, so he turned back toward town. Sheriff Dodd would want to talk with him again soon. He needed to see about getting some of his things replaced and tend to the livery horses in their temporary quarters at the black-smith's. He would talk to Great-Aunt Deborah, too. She was his relation and possessed a godly spirit and kind heart. She would have advice for him.

Seeing Dodd ahead of him, Ben lengthened his stride and caught up with the lawman. "Have you come up with a plan?"

Dodd jumped. "Don't sneak up on a body like that." He faced Ben. "I was looking for you. I do have a plan. Some of us will stand guard over the livery and see if anyone comes to search the ashes."

"Not tonight."

Ben wanted to talk to Great-Aunt Deborah, and standing guard would prevent him doing so if he needed to be there at dusk.

"Yep, tonight."

"But the ashes will still be hot inside."

"All the more reason to stand guard. Stop any fires from starting again."

With the heavy rain that began in the afternoon, no fire had a chance. But Ben, Matt, and the sheriff hid in strategic locations around the site of the livery.

They got nothing during the vigil except cold and wet. Ben woke late the next day, sneezing and chilled. He let Great-Aunt Deborah cosset him through the morning, but as idleness made him uneasy, he prepared for another night's vigil.

"You shouldn't go out there again," Great-Aunt Deborah advised over dinner. "You haven't seen Lily since the fire."

Ben began to clear the table of dishes. "This has to be done and can't wait."

"Talking to Lily shouldn't wait, either."

Ben's stomach clenched. "So she did decide to go?"

"That's not for me to discuss with you." Great-Aunt Deborah compressed her lips, but her eyes twinkled.

Her reaction bemusing him, Ben said good night and left the house.

For the first three hours of a blessedly warm and dry night, nothing stirred in the ashes except the wind. Then the crunch of a footfall on the gravel of the stable yard alerted Ben to an intruder approaching. Ben stood motionless beneath the overhang of the blacksmith shop roof. Motionless and poised for action. Stars and a three-quarter moon illuminated the site enough for him to make out a shadow slipping to the edge of the burned timbers and walls.

Careful not to make any noise, Ben closed in on the man. From the corner of his eye, he caught movement indicating that Dodd moved in on the intruder, too.

"Now!" Dodd shouted.

He and Ben grabbed the man's arms.

"Yieeee!" He shrieked like an angry cat and lashed out with his feet.

"Don't move," Dodd commanded. "You're under arrest for trespassing and likely burning down the livery."

"No, no," squeaked Jake Doerfel. "I'm getting a story."

"In the middle of the night?"

For once, Ben appreciated the lawman's sarcasm.

"You could've gotten all the story you liked when you helped fight this blaze you started."

"I didn't start it." Jake tugged against Ben's hold. "I have no reason to do anything so foolish."

"Except look for gold," Ben said in the

man's ear.

"Gold? What gold?" Jake's voice grew higher with each word. "I don't want anything to do with gold."

"You'd been reading all the back issues of the paper about the gold."

Jake kicked Ben's shin. "Shut your mouth about that."

"No matter," Dodd drawled. "We can all figure out you have all those old newspapers to read, too. You likely know more'n anyone else about the gold."

"No, no. I–I'm . . ." Suddenly he slumped in their hold. "It's my gold. Doerfel isn't my name. It's Mitchell. Jim Mitchell was my father, but he got himself killed without telling me where he hid the gold. But I'm going to find it. It's mine. It's mine." His voice broke on a sob.

"It belongs to the government," Dodd corrected. "And this livery belonged to Mr. Gilchrist. You destroyed it to find something that isn't yours."

"Or might not be there," Ben added.

"It is. It is. . . ."

Jake continued his protests all the way to the one cell the town called a jail.

"Do you think it really is in those ashes?" Matt asked.

"I don't know." Dodd rubbed a knuckle

across his chin. "But we're gonna look."

The next day, they looked. Half the town turned out to help. Ben didn't see Lily, but she would be at the telegraph office. She would have enjoyed the festive atmosphere. People laughed and joked and gladly got their hands and clothes dirty moving ash-laden planks. The air crackled with excitement, and Ben's heart raced harder with each layer of the building they uncovered.

Each empty layer.

They found scraps of harness leather and canvas, twisted iron from buggy wheels and farm equipment. Nothing, right down to the earth below the foundation, resembled so much as the melted remains of gold.

FOURTEEN

"I still can't believe someone would destroy his life over the chance at finding gold." Lily faced Ben across Mrs. Twining's kitchen table, seeing him for the first time since the fire. "Or worse, risk your life."

"The prospect of easy money makes people do strange and dangerous things." Ben rested his hands on the table. "But I'm safe."

"I am thankful for that." Lily smiled and fell silent.

Ben smiled back, but neither of them looked directly at one another. As the coffee steamed and the smell of a dried apple pie filled the kitchen, silence between them grew. Lily had so much to say to him that she didn't know where to start. She knew Ben wanted to talk to her, too. He had walked her home from the telegraph office, giving her that excuse, yet had said nothing of what lay on his mind. While she made dinner and the pie, he talked with his aunt. During the meal, the three of them discussed the fire and Jake Doerfel's attempts to find the gold. Now, alone for the first time since Saturday, they talked about Jake again, repeating what they had said earlier.

Lily wondered if she should speak up first. She'd always understood that the man brought up the subject of a relationship between a lady and himself, but maybe his odd upbringing hadn't taught him such things.

Maybe she should start, give him a nudge — or push — with her announcement.

She clasped the edge of the table. "Ben, I want to tell you about my job —"

"Lily, I want to tell you about my decision," he said at the same time.

They looked at each other and laughed.

"You go first." They spoke at the same time again.

"Ladies first," Ben pronounced.

"All right." Lily took a deep breath. Her heart pounded against her ribs, tapping out a Morse code of apprehension. "I turned down the job offer."

"Lily." He swallowed. "You're staying?"

"Yes."

"Why?"

"Because . . ."

The words "I love you" stuck in her throat. She didn't think she was supposed to say so before he declared his intentions toward her.

"This is where I want to stay." She gave him another part of the answer. "And where I believe the Lord wants me to stay. I was never at peace about taking the job in the city. I have peace about this decision. I don't need all the noise and people to be happy."

"I'm glad to hear it." He gave her a half smile, not an indication of joy at her announcement. "Though I've taken over your room."

"I can stay with Mrs. Willoughby or move to the boardinghouse."

Smelling a crust beginning to brown too much, Lily rose to remove the pie from the oven. She kept her back to him so he couldn't read her disappointment in his lack of enthusiasm for her remaining in Browning City.

"You should stay with family," she concluded.

"I wasn't going to continue living here in town." His voice was tight. "With everything that happened, things like my not having work at the livery now that it's burned down and not having a place to live made me think maybe the Lord wanted me to move on. I thought I had misunderstood what He wanted for me because I wanted it so much. But you seem to understand that."

"I do." She set the pie on the table, still without looking at him. "Sometimes I think we want something so much, we let ourselves believe it's what God wants for us." She picked up the coffeepot and faced him at last. "What will you do now that the livery is gone? Is Mr. Gilchrist going to rebuild?"

Am I any part of that life?

"He is. He still wants me to manage it, and he wants me to manage the store, too."

"Ben, that's wonderful!"

She wished she had the right to hug him.

She set down the coffeepot and reached for a knife to cut the pie.

He covered her hand with his. "Wait, please." He gazed into her eyes.

What she read there made her sink onto the nearest chair, her heart beating so hard she could scarcely breathe. Tenderness. Love. Longing. Everything she felt for him.

"Lily, may I be so bold as to ask if another reason you're staying here is because you care for me?"

"Yes. I mean, yes, you may ask, and yes, it's true." She reached for her coffee cup, realized it was still empty, and picked up his to wash the dryness from her throat. "I knew the night of the fire I wanted to stay near you."

"I was ready to leave here to be near you."

Then ask me to marry you.

She squeezed his hand, trying to convey the message to him without saying it.

"I would like — love — a future with you, Lily." A tremor ran through his fingers. "It's possible. That is, if you're interested enough, but . . ." He paused.

Lily bit back a shriek of frustration.

"I'm going to make good wages soon, and I have my savings." He continued his speech, avoiding her gaze again. "But I still don't feel I can ask you to marry me before I have a home for us."

She shouldn't have stayed in Browning City. Chicago would have offered them dozens of places to live once he had a job. But Browning City had nothing other than rooms to rent, not a good way to start married life.

Except . . .

"The livery?" Hope ran through her.

"When I accepted the job offer from Mr. Gilchrist this morning, I told him we shouldn't build quarters behind the livery. Too dangerous with needing to have a stove and all."

"You told him not to —" Lily stood and

backed from the table. "He was going to? And you told him not to?"

"Yes, but —"

"We could have had a place to be together, but you prevented it?"

Ben sighed. "Lily, when I thought seriously about it, I knew I couldn't take my bride back to a room that forever smells like horses. You wouldn't like that."

"You didn't ask me if I would or would not." Tears stung her eyes. "Excuse me." She swung toward the door.

"No, wait." In a flash, he stood between her and the door. "I'm going about this all wrong. I'm trying to ask you if you'll wait for me."

"How long?" The flirtatious question slipped out before she could stop herself.

He frowned, but a twinkle sparked in his eyes. "Possibly for as long as you plan to love me."

"Is that all?" She touched her fingertips to his cheek. "Then it's only for as long as you plan to love me."

"That's a long time." He cradled her hand with his. "Something like forever."

"Lily." Becky flung herself into Lily's arms before church on Sunday. "Matt asked me to marry him. I know we haven't been courting all that long, but we've known each other for ages, and he's so good and kind, and his parents are letting us have their house and — isn't it wonderful?"

"Truly."

Lily hugged her friend. She was happy for Becky, though the sight of Ben on the other side of the sanctuary, talking with Jackson Reeves, sent her heart into a confused spiral of joy and sorrow.

No matter what she said to him, he refused to propose to her until he could offer her a real home.

"So I need to buy yards and yards of lace from you." Becky linked her arm with Lily's. "Momma says I can have a whole new dress if I don't buy too much fabric for it, so I thought maybe lots of lace instead of a wide skirt."

"Make your skirt as wide as you like. I have yards of lace made. I'll give it to you."

"But what about the bazaar?"

Lily shrugged. "It's mostly just crocheted collars and cuffs I sell there."

Becky winked. "But what about your own wedding dress?"

"We don't have anywhere to live."

Although the fact hurt her, she experienced only a twinge of envy for her friend's blessing of a fiancé who could provide her with a proper home. The Lord knew what He wanted for her and Ben. He would provide. If He did not provide . . .

Lily didn't think that far. Her faith grew daily, but it still had its limitations. The prospect of a future without Ben as her husband hurt too much to contemplate.

"Someone in Browning City should build houses they can rent to people like you two and newcomers." Becky began tugging Lily toward Matt, who had joined Ben and Pastor Jackson. "Don't big cities have houses to rent?"

"Yes, I think they do. But we live here, and we plan to stay here."

"You can't believe how happy I am about that." Becky paused. "I couldn't imagine Browning City without you here stirring things up."

Lily frowned. "I hope I brought more than that to town."

"Browning City without you, Lily, would be like summer without sunshine." Becky grinned. "Is that good enough for you?"

"Better than good enough." Lily laughed, once again assured staying was right.

Even her frustration over the town having nowhere Ben and she could live made her doubt her decision only once or twice in the next week. Mostly, she was too busy finishing up preparations for the spring bazaar and anticipating the plowing contest. If Ben won, they could buy land and build a house. Yet she didn't know how he could win. Although he had rescued the plow from the fire, it had gotten scorched. It was also old and heavy, not like one of the improved John Deere plows some farmers had. Ben was young and strong, yet she wasn't certain he had as much experience as others did.

"God knows what He wants for us," she told herself each time she grew uncertain.

Part of her hoped it wasn't a farm miles from town. She doubted she would ever be satisfied with few to no neighbors near enough for anything from spontaneous dinners together to borrowing a cup of sugar. She felt her gift for organizing people to get things done could better be used in town than out, and she kept telling herself to let God have that talent for His glory, not her own.

Whatever her future, she employed every bit of her skill up to the minute the bazaar opened. Held outside town to have enough space and have a field for the contest close by, the fair of booths celebrated all the skills farm- and townsfolk employed during the more idle winter months. More barter than exchange of coin took place, but because everyone paid for a booth, the community received money. This year, everyone worked hard to raise funds for a library. The previous year, they had raised money for a church hall.

Lily had taken only cash the previous year, her first to participate. She didn't intend to carry on the same practice this year. She'd felt no need for antimacassars, quilts, and frilly aprons before. That had all changed.

She understood the meaning behind the words "hope chest."

By the end of the first day, she didn't have a crocheted collar or cuff left. Her box held some coins and numerous linens, exquisitely stitched by ladies who took pride in their work. She had even exchanged a length of lace for a colorful rag rug.

One day, she would have her own floor on which to spread it.

Without any goods to sell the next day, she helped Becky, Eva, and the others with their toffee; then she closed up shop and walked arm in arm with the other women to the edge of the field.

"Are Matt and Tom joining us?" she asked them.

"They're referees." Eva glanced at the line of plows across from them. "This field is stonier than I remember from when I came two years ago."

"I think Iowa grows as many stones as it does crops." Becky giggled. "One year, when Mr. Deere himself came, a man plowed up a rock so big his blade bent."

Eva made a face. "I hope it wasn't the blade of a John Deere plow."

"It wasn't, and he pointed that out, of — oh, there's Matt." Becky waved.

Even across a field, Lily saw Matt's face light up. She wondered how she had ever thought he would care for her, or she for him. She scarcely thought of him now.

She had scarcely thought of him since meeting Ben.

Ben stood a hundred feet or so from Matt. He squatted before his plow, tinkering with something she couldn't see from this distance.

She shaded her eyes with her hand. "Is everything all right?"

"You worry too much." Becky slipped her arm around Lily's waist. "He'll do fine. Even third place is good."

Eva held up her hand. "Hush, they're about to start."

Sheriff Dodd stepped forward and read from a sheet of paper. Lily couldn't hear the words, only his sonorous voice, but presumed he pronounced the rules. When he finished his speech, he stepped behind the line of men and plows, picked a rifle up from the ground, and fired into the air.

The three ladies jumped, laughed, and started to cheer Ben on. All around them, ladies called for their men to do well, and children ran about, shouting for their daddies.

Only in the Iowa countryside, Lily couldn't help thinking, *would an entire town turn out to watch grown men pull plows across a field. Never would city folk do something so silly.*

Or with so much togetherness and fun.

Even if Ben didn't win, the bazaar and contest were worth every minute with her friends.

Her family.

Filled with love for the women beside her, she hugged both of them.

"I know." Becky hugged her back. "I'm worried, too."

"About what?" Lily blinked, glanced back at the field, and understood.

Ben was faltering. No, not him, his plow.

"He hit a rock." Eva narrowed her eyes against the glare of the noonday sun. "The blade is uneven now."

"Oh no, that takes off points if the furrows aren't straight," Becky wailed. "It's just not fair."

"It's not." Lily's heart sank into her middle.

She started to pray.

Ben kept going, but he fell far behind half the other men. In no way could he win.

Lily clenched her hands and tried to pray. She was so sure the Lord wanted them together. She didn't know how He could give her peace about staying in Browning City, even make her happy about it, then keep her and Ben apart.

I can't bear to see him day after day and stay mere friends.

But of course she would if the Lord wanted her to.

I accept this, Lord.

"I wonder if the plow was damaged in the fire," Eva mused. "It just doesn't look right. See that crack?"

Lily and Becky shook their heads.

"You have remarkable eyesight." Lily leaned forward, squinting. "I can't see a — oh, yes, I can."

A groove formed along the side of the plow. She also noticed the crease between Ben's eyes and tightness of his chin.

"Another rock might break it."

As Becky spoke, the blade struck another rock. The frame shuddered. The groove turned into a fissure. While the other contestants continued, Ben stopped and turned to his equipment.

"That's an odd sight." Eva headed onto the field. "Come on, you two. Something peculiar is happening here."

"What?" Lily noticed nothing too out of the ordinary.

"Something in the crack." Eva tossed the cryptic remark over her shoulder.

"What?" Lily followed Eva and Becky along Ben's lane. Matt and Tom gestured to them to go back. The ladies ignored the men and continued.

"Ben," Becky called, "what happened?"

He stood beside the plow, pulling on something protruding from the crack. Concentration etched his face, and when he glanced at them, excitement sparkled in his eyes.

"This plow was never intended to be used for this purpose again." He yanked on what appeared to be a scrap of fabric. "It's been cobbled together —"

"What are you all doing?" Matt demanded, Tom right behind him.

"You're supposed to be judging the contest," Eva said.

"It's done." Tom frowned at her. "The Hastings lad won. They're all headed this way."

They were. Lily glanced around to see what appeared to be the entire town swarming toward them.

"I need a chisel," Ben said.

Someone ran for tent stakes and a hammer. Ben and Tom used the stakes to form wedges to pry the pieces of the plow apart far enough for Ben to extract a canvas bag.

A canvas bag that sagged in his hand.

"Let me have that." Sheriff Dodd stepped up beside Ben. "Hidden like that, it's probably contraband of some kind."

"I believe it is," Ben said. "This plow used to belong to Jim Mitchell."

Gasps rose from the crowd like a wave.

Lily opened her mouth, but no sound emerged. She met Ben's gaze, and both of them grinned.

"Ladies and gentlemen," Dodd announced, staring into the bag, "Mr. Purcell is right in his surmise. He has indeed found the gold."

FIFTEEN

REGARDING YOUR LETTER STOP
PURCELL WILL RECEIVE REWARD STOP
WILL DELIVER IN PERSON STOP

Scarcely able to breathe, Lily read the telegram addressed to Sheriff Dodd and signed by a general in Washington City. She wanted to dash from the telegraph office and race into town, shouting the news all the way — and more.

"We can build our house now."

But she could say nothing to anyone other than the sheriff. He would have the privilege of telling Ben.

The sooner he received the news, the better.

She slid off her stool and yanked open the door. "Theo?" She waved the telegram at him. "Please deliver this at once, and don't you dare read it."

"No, Miss Lily, you know I can't deliver

telegrams right now. Afternoon train's due any minute."

"But this is important."

"Is it, now?" Theo grinned. "Maybe you should take it yourself."

"You know I can't leave the office until Toby gets here."

"And he's slower'n the train in an ice storm." Theo peered down the road. "No sign of him."

"He isn't late yet."

He wasn't due for another quarter hour. By the time he arrived and she got into town, Dodd would have left his office. She would have to hunt him down.

She chafed at the delay then laughed at herself. They had waited two months to hear if Ben would indeed receive the reward for the gold. They should be able to wait another hour or more. Of course, who knew when the general would arrive with the money. The sum the sheriff had mentioned staggered her. They could build a fine house with it.

They could also buy a farm, and the notion of it still gave Lily pause. She knew Ben still wanted land, lots of it, and that piece along the river was still for sale. Lily kept telling herself it wasn't too far from town, not too far from others. Doing so didn't help much. She felt comfortable being alone now, yet preferred not to be, and still doubted her ability to remain content as the wife of a farmer.

Often during the last two months, she'd thought perhaps she should tell Ben to find a lady who wanted to be a farm wife, feeding chickens and milking cows, slopping pigs and preserving vegetables.

Well, she liked the preserving part.

Now that everything looked as though it would work out for them, Lily stared at her telegraph machine, waiting for Toby to arrive, and wondered if maybe she didn't love Ben enough to marry him no matter where they lived. She had told him she would love him all her life, but if she couldn't be happy regardless of their circumstances, she might be mistaken.

Her insides knotted, she greeted Toby, grabbed the telegram, and headed for Dodd's office as fast as she could manage and remain ladylike. Through the window, she saw him seated at his desk, inspecting wanted posters.

"In case any of these men come through my town," he told her, stacking the posters. "How may I help you, Miss Lily?"

"Telegram." She handed it to him.

He read it and let out a low whistle. "The

general himself. Well, what do you know? Guess I should run along and tell Ben."

"Please do." Lily hugged her arms across her middle. "He'll be at the store."

"Yes, ma'am." Dodd grinned. "And let me be the first one to congratulate you."

"For what, sir?"

Dodd guffawed. "For what indeed. You go home and make yourself pretty. I expect you'll have a caller later."

Laughing, Lily did as he suggested. She combed and pinned up her hair. She tucked a fresh collar around her neckline. She sat on the front porch to catch the warm air of the late afternoon and waited.

Thirty minutes passed. They felt like thirty hours. She reviewed Dodd's words and realized how embarrassed Ben and she would be if they didn't marry. Everyone expected them to tie the knot. She expected them to marry soon — had even made her wedding dress without telling anyone other than Becky and Eva, who were sworn to secrecy. She didn't think she was being presumptive, but now that the moment had arrived, Ben might have other plans.

"I want my farm to prosper first," she imagined him saying. "You said you'd wait for me."

She had said something of the kind. Silly

female for making such a promise. No telling what notion he would come up with to postpone their union.

Because he was as scared as she was?

Lily shot to her feet, preparing to hide in her room.

She saw Ben striding toward her and sat down again.

He bounded up the steps to Mrs. Willoughby's porch and dropped onto the seat beside her. He sounded winded, as though he had run all the way, and carried the aromas of the store with him — cinnamon, cloves, and fresh coffee. She inhaled the rich fragrances and waited for him to speak.

"I just got some good news." He laughed. "You already know, though, don't you?"

"I do." She beamed at him. "Congratulations. And a general's coming to deliver it himself."

"Not *is* coming." Ben shook his head. "He's here. Came in on the train. Seems he's bought a farm here to live on with his family when he leaves the military, so he offered to deliver the reward in person."

"He bought a farm here for his old age?" Lily couldn't keep the astonishment from her tone. "Where is it?"

Ben gazed at the maple tree in Mrs. Willoughby's front yard. "The piece of land we visited in April."

"The one you wanted?"

"Yes." His voice remained neutral.

"Why, Ben, that's . . . um . . ."

She stumbled over saying it was terrible news. For her, it wasn't terrible at all.

"It's not too bad." Ben stretched his long legs ahead of him as though settling in for a lengthy chat. "I found another property about fifteen miles out."

"Fifteen?" Lily's voice squeaked.

She gripped the edge of her chair, reminding herself all would be well when she was married to the man she loved, the mate the Lord had found for her.

"Of course, it's got to be cleared and tilled. Lots of rocks." Ben shrugged. "I figure in a year or two we should be able to build something there."

"A year or two?" Lily frowned at him. "That's a long time, isn't it?"

"Not when compared with forev—" His voice broke, and he started to laugh. "Lily, don't look so horrified. I'm teasing you."

"You're not buying land that far from town?" She turned toward him.

Love and laughter filled his eyes. "No, my dear. I'm buying the store and the livery from Mr. Gilchrist."

"But your farm. You wanted it more than

anything."

"So much that I knew I had to give it up. And when the opportunity came along to buy the business and have a wife who prefers town, I knew what I was supposed to be doing." He leaned toward her and grasped her hand. "That is, if you'll be my wife."

"You know I will."

He leaned forward and kissed her in front of anyone who might be watching.

"How soon can you put a wedding together?"

"I can have a wedding ready in a week. How soon can you build us a house?"

EPILOGUE

They waited to marry for another three months until after harvest so everyone could attend the wedding, including the general turning farmer and his family. Lily wore the dress she had finished making in June. Rather than trimming the gown with yards of lace, she had plied her needles to fashioning a lace veil. It floated around her as she walked down the aisle of the church, making her feel as though she drifted through a dream.

But everything was wonderfully real, from the rows of friends and neighbors on either side of her to the man waiting for her at the altar. Sunlight shone on his face, and she wondered how she could have once thought she wouldn't follow him anywhere the Lord led them.

When she reached his side, she slipped her hand into his and said, "I will."

"So will I." Ben grinned down at her.

The pastor chuckled. "You're getting ahead of me," he whispered.

"But it's good to see a bride and groom so sure of what they're doing." Aloud, he added, "Now for all of the ceremony."

Lily knew she and Ben gave the right responses but didn't remember much else about it. Ben and she had already spoken their vows before God in their first, simple words to each other.

She didn't recall much of the festivities following the wedding, either. For once, no one had let her plan or prepare a thing. Eva, Becky, and Mary had taken over so Lily could see to more important things, like decorating their new home.

She expected to return there after the wedding, but Ben led her out of the church hall to a chorus of good wishes and lifted her into the livery's new buggy.

"We can walk," she protested.

"No we can't." Ben jumped up beside her. "We aren't even driving ourselves."

"But —"

Matt climbed in and took up the reins. "Keep her close to you, Ben."

"Where are we going?" Lily asked.

Ben tucked her close to his side. "The train depot."

"Train?" Lily nearly jumped up and down

with excitement. "We're going on a train? Where?"

"Chicago." Ben rested his cheek against the top of her head. "I thought you might like an adventure before you become a staid matron in a small town."

Just as she knew she would enjoy their honeymoon in a real city, Lily knew life with Ben would be the best adventure she would ever live.

ABOUT THE AUTHOR

Award-winning author **Laurie Alice Eakes** has always loved books. When she ran out of available stories to entertain and encourage her, she began creating her own tales of love and adventure. In 2006, she celebrated the publication of her first hardcover novel. Much to her astonishment and delight, it won the National Readers Choice Award. Besides writing, she teaches classes to other writers, mainly on research, something she enjoys nearly as much as creating characters and their exploits. A graduate of Asbury College and Seton Hill University, she lives in Northern Virginia with her husband and sundry animals.